Out of the Dark

Kathleen Farnum Aldrich

Illustrated by Keith Neeley

Bob Jones University Press, Greenville, South Carolina 29614

Library of Congress Cataloging-in-Publication Data

Aldrich, Kathleen, 1923-
    Out of the dark / Kathleen Aldrich.
        p.   cm.
    Summary: Paralyzed and grief-stricken after surviving the auto ac-
cident which killed her parents, twelve-year-old Christie deals with her
problems with the help of her grandparents, doctor, friends, and God.
    ISBN 0-89084-799-1
    [1. Physically handicapped—Fiction.   2. Christian life—Fiction.]
I. Title.
PZ7.A36850u 1994
[Fic]—dc20   94–48662
                                                                  CIP
                                                                   AC

Excerpt from FOR SPEECH SAKE! by Ruth E. Jones
Copyright © 1970 Reprinted by permission of Pitman Learning, Inc.,
Belmont, CA 94002

Out of the Dark

Edited by Suzette Jordan
Cover and illustrations by Keith Neely

© 1995 Bob Jones University Press
Greenville, South Carolina 29614

ISBN 0-89084-799-1

15   14   13   12   11   10   9   8   7   6   5   4   3   2   1

In the beginning: Allyson

The Good News: Patricia, Dot,

and her twenty-six children

Revelation: Elizabeth

Contents

1

The Dream

This must be a nightmare. Christie opened her eyes and tried to turn her head. It wouldn't move. Ahead, she saw an unfamiliar wall, painted pink. She opened her mouth to say, "What's going on here?" Not a word came out.

Perhaps, if she closed her eyes and opened them again, she'd be in her own room with the pine needle wallpaper she'd picked out herself. On the side wall, twin windows with sunshine yellow curtains would brighten the room.

She stared down the length of the bed. That wasn't her footboard, made of maple wood. It was very short, tan and metal, with something taped to the top; she couldn't make out what it was. Sweat made her body feel clammy, and she was rattling the bed with her shaking.

The bedspread was white and thin, like a sheet, and smoothed over the two humps that must be her legs. Her feet were sticking straight up, not covered, and they were shut into high black sneakers, like boxers wore on television. She must be in a nightmare. What if someone should see those weird feet?

Now Christie's heart was thumping. She looked at the wide window to her left; its sill was covered with greeting cards, standing open. The dark blue curtains were limp, their color one she'd never choose for her room. In the wall space between the window and the corner stood a tan chest of drawers that matched the bed. She couldn't see herself in the mirror that was screwed to the pink wall above the chest. If this really were a dream, she probably wouldn't be herself anyway.

It was time to yell for Mom. She opened her mouth again, but not a sound came out. The dream went on. She closed her eyes. Maybe the next time she opened them she'd be back in her room where she belonged.

When she opened her eyes again, she could see Grandpa and Grandma MacLane at the foot of the bed, holding hands and laughing; they had tears in their eyes. They must have come early for Christmas, after all. Her heart quieted.

They walked to opposite sides of the bed, bent down, and kissed her. Christie tried to say, "What's the matter?"

"Don't try to talk, darling," Grandma told her. "With that tube in your neck, you can't—"

Grandpa made a face at Grandma, like some kind of signal, and she stopped.

Christie tried to touch her neck, but the hand ignored her and just lay there. The thumping started again. At that moment she realized that the pink room was in a hospital. Why was she here?

Grandma reached over Christie's pillow and lifted something on a long cord; she heard a distant buzz. A nurse wearing a clean white uniform came into the room. She was young, and her black hair was short under the white cap with the black stripe. Her eyes were very blue. At this moment, they were sparkling and excited.

"Well, look who's back!" she said, taking the buzzer out of Grandma's hand and pressing it herself. The door opened and more nurses looked in, laughing and grinning enough to break their faces.

"Page Dr. Alexander—tell him to hurry," said the nurse.

A tall young man in a green jacket ran in and looked down at Christie. "You're beautiful!" he said. He bent down and kissed her, smack on the forehead. It made her feel odd. She didn't know any of those people. This dream was getting sillier all the time. She squeezed her eyes shut. If only Mom and Dad would come in and shake her awake to tell her, "It's just a dream, honey."

Far away, Christie heard words, words, words, but she couldn't open her eyes; they were too heavy.

Grandma MacLane was saying, "Theodore! We have to tell her, as soon as she opens her eyes again. The sooner she knows, the sooner she can begin adjusting to it."

"When she asks is soon enough," Grandpa said. Christie could hear Grandma blowing her nose. She must be crying again.

Whatever it was, Christie wasn't going to ask. She'd better not know something so serious that it made them argue and made Grandma cry. She wished she could close her ears when she closed her eyes.

More voices, first the tall doctor's, then the young nurse's. They were leaning over her, but the heavy things on her eyelids wouldn't let her open them.

"Christie! Christie! Can you hear me, Christie?" That was the doctor's voice. More sniffles from Grandma.

"Why don't you two go down to the coffee shop while Dr. Alexander removes the tube and checks Christie over?" The nurse's voice asked a question, but it sounded as if she expected to be obeyed. Christie heard the whoosh of the door as it opened and then swung shut.

"Okay, sweetheart, this will feel strange for a minute, but it won't hurt." Christie felt cool fingers against her throat, then a smarting and a pulling sensation. Just as she thought she ought to groan, to tell the doctor she was scared, he said, "Fine. That will be better just as soon as I get this tape on right."

Christie lay very still and waited. "It's all done. Whenever you are ready, you can talk." The man's voice stopped, as if he were waiting.

If she made a mighty effort, Christie thought she could open her eyes. She concentrated on them. "Eyes, eyes, eyes, eyes," she said in her head, over and over again. First, she felt her eyelids twitch, then slowly, they lifted.

"Aren't those the brightest blue eyes you've ever seen?" asked Dr. Alexander. "Miss Whitaker, come over here and say 'Good morning' to Christie."

"Hi, sugar!" The nurse's face beamed down at her. "You're wrong about the eyes, though. I'd call them violet. Definitely violet!"

"Don't worry, Christie," the doctor said. "You'll be talking before long. I think I'll call you Miss Van Winkle."

Why would he want to call her that?

When Grandma and Grandpa came back, Grandpa grinned down at her and put his hand on her shoulder, patting it a little.

As the doctor left the room, he motioned to Grandpa and Grandma to follow him into the hall. Christie couldn't hear what they talked about, but the drone of their voices went on for a long time before they came back to the room. Grandma's eyes were red and wet again, and she dabbed her nose with a blue tissue.

"You know how your grandmother is, Christie," Grandpa said. "She always has to cry, especially when she's happy."

She doesn't *look* happy, Christie thought.

Grandpa kept talking. "I'll bet you've been wondering about those sporty sneakers." Christie watched his face. "When you were sleeping, your feet kept falling over because the muscles got tired. Dr. Alexander said those sneakers would help the muscles out. How about that?"

She stared at the ugly black things.

Grandpa understood. "We'll cover those up, right now." He rolled the sheet, blanket, and bedspread down over the foot of the bed, leaving them loose, so they wouldn't bend her feet. The two mounds looked a little better than the sneakers.

Grandma had stopped sniffling; now she was fussing with the cards and picking leaves off a plant on the windowsill. All that made Christie tired. She closed her eyes and slept again.

"Christie! Christie! Wake up! I have something for you to drink. No more needles for you. Isn't that too bad!" Miss Whitaker was beside the bed, Grandpa and Grandma were not in the room, and Christie's eyes opened with no trouble at all. The nurse had rolled a tray stand over Christie's stomach and had pressed a button that lifted the back of the bed so she was halfway sitting up. Eggnog? She didn't like that stuff!

But her tongue was dry, and the thought of something cool to drink appealed to her. Miss Whitaker put a plastic straw into her mouth, one that bent with little wrinkles, like Mom's vacuum cleaner tube. "Slow now. Take it slow."

She sucked on the straw and the cold eggnog flowed over her tongue and down her throat. Then she coughed, dragging in a big breath. Nothing worked right!

"A little at a time. We don't want you to choke. Ready now? Just a little sip this time." The nurse held the glass in one hand and the straw between two fingers of the other. She put it against Christie's lips. This time, she was very careful. One small sip. It was *good*. And she'd thought she didn't like eggnog. It took a long time to finish, so long that Christie's eyelids were heavy before the glass was empty.

Miss Whitaker pressed the button that lowered the back of the bed, plumped up the pillow, and pulled the sheet tight under Christie. She folded the top sheet over the blanket, tucking them under Christie's arms. She cocked her head. "Who covered your feet?"

Christie expected her to snatch the bedspread off the sneakers, but the nurse looked at her for a few seconds, then she said, "Okay, you win! I'll be back after your nap." She left the room. Again, Christie slept.

Each time she woke up, she was more alert. No longer was she surprised to find herself in the pink hospital room. Once the door opened and a gray-haired woman in a blue jacket came in. "Hi! I'm Ellen, the therapist. I know you very well because I've seen you and exercised you many times. Do you remember?" Christie didn't.

And she didn't like the exercises. They hurt after a few lifts of her legs and feet. When the therapist didn't stop, Christie felt like kicking her. She groaned.

"You don't like that, do you?" said Ellen. "Believe it or not, I'm glad it hurts. That means your muscles are working, and someday you'll move them all by yourself. Come on, hand, you're next." Ellen laughed.

Christie didn't think it was funny. If her muscles ever came back, she'd fix that therapist. She was glad when Ellen left her alone and she could sleep. In her dream, Mom and Dad had come to take her home. Eight-year-old Benjamin was waiting in the back seat of the car, his arm around their big dog, Rusty. When she got in, Rusty wiggled all over like a puppy and licked her hands with his warm, wet tongue. Mom and Dad sat in the front, the motor started, and the car rounded a curve to go onto the interstate highway. Looking back out of her window, Christie could see the trailer truck catching up to them, too fast. Much too fast! She screamed, but no sound came out of her mouth.

Grandma was leaning over her, and Christie could feel the tears running down her cheeks. How would she ever know what was real and what was a dream? She was back in the pink room. Her grandmother was crying again. Where was Grandpa? Maybe he'd gone home to sit with Benjamin so Mom and Dad could come and stay with her. She hoped so.

But when Grandpa came into the room, he was with Dr. Alexander and Miss Whitaker. The doctor sat on the edge of the bed and lifted Christie's hand. "You remembered, didn't you?" he asked.

Christie let the tears flow. She couldn't stop them, even if she wanted to. For once, Grandma wasn't crying. She took

Christie's other hand and squeezed it hard. Grandpa held her sneakered feet, one in each hand. They didn't have to tell her. She knew Mom and Dad would never be coming to stay with her. She wished she could block her ears. She didn't want to hear them talk about Benjamin and Rusty, either. They were all gone. She was alone.

Dr. Alexander said, "Look at me, Christie. Benjamin is well. He's in California with your aunt and uncle. I understand he has five cousins to keep him company. Rusty is staying with your friend Brenda until you're well enough to get him. Are you listening to me? You are *not* alone. Your grandparents will take you home just as soon as you're ready to leave the hospital. Now, it's time for a good rest; then we'll talk some more, okay?"

Miss Whitaker gave her a shot to make her sleepy again, but Christie didn't even feel the needle.

2

Miss Van Winkle

All the days were the same. Nurses came and went, Grandpa and Grandma sat with her, and Christie just lay and looked at the walls. She did not talk, and the only times she moved were when the nurses turned her over or fed her. Ellen, the gray-haired therapist, moved her legs and feet, her hands and arms. Even though it hurt, it didn't make her mad anymore. She didn't care.

Grandma cried a lot, but Christie didn't. Grandpa told her something new each day. She couldn't ask questions, but he talked to her as though she had.

"Christie, it's April. The crocuses are coming up and the forsythia is in bloom. Next week, we'll celebrate your birthday."

Her birthday? Why, it had been weeks and weeks before her birthday when the accident happened!

Sometimes Grandma fussed with Christie's hair. Why? One day, Grandpa told her she'd had her hair shaved off for an operation while she was asleep. Then he'd given her a hand mirror so she could see herself. He explained her long sleep, only he called it a coma. When she saw her short, fuzzy hair, she closed her eyes. She was ugly. Fuzz and black sneakers! Good thing Brenda couldn't see her now.

Grandpa said she looked cute with her new hair style, and he brought her a soft brush that Grandma used every day to fluff the fuzz.

Her grandparents hinted at a birthday surprise. It didn't matter. She remembered Mom's cakes, each year better than the last. Celebrations were just for family—no big parties with yelling kids, like some she'd been invited to. She even loved Benjamin's birthday, on Halloween. But California was too far away to share their days.

Why did she feel so angry all the time? She was angriest at God for letting that accident happen, and she was angry at Mom and Dad for leaving her all alone. And what was the matter with that doctor? Why hadn't he made her well? It wasn't fair! She felt like screaming, like kicking off the bedclothes and running out of here. Everyone kept smiling and saying funny things to her. Didn't they know they made her angry? She wanted to go home.

Today must be her birthday, because this morning Grandpa and Grandma brought in presents, all wrapped in colored paper. Someone else had to open them. What fun was that? Pajamas, slippers, bathrobe, note paper, pen, a fancy sweater, puzzle books, and a crazy silk jacket to wear in bed. She looked at each one as Grandpa or Grandma held it up. There wasn't one thing for a kid to do when she was on her feet!

Dr. Alexander came in with some nurses, Miss Whitaker carried in a birthday cake on a tray, and everyone sang. Christie stared at the burning candles and the fat pink and blue roses that covered the cake. It looked like the ones she'd seen at the bakery. There were paper plates and plastic forks, and Grandpa poked bits of cake into Christie's mouth. It was dry and hard to swallow. After three bites, she pressed her lips together and wouldn't open them.

She didn't even have enough breath to blow out the twelve candles. Five of them flickered on after she blew. Lucky she hadn't bothered to make a wish. It would never come true anyway. She closed her eyes and tried to shut out the cheerful sounds all around her. Nobody cared. She knew she didn't.

Where was the great surprise Grandpa had mentioned?

She opened her eyes again when she felt someone lean close to her. Dr. Alexander had brought her a paperback book. The cover, bordered with blue, had a picture of a black horse rearing up on its hind legs; the costumed rider had no head. He held a jack-o'-lantern high above his shoulders. The title said *Washington Irving's Sketch Book.*

"Miss Van Winkle, there's a special story in here and I'm going to read it to you for your birthday," said the doctor. "Later, you can read the rest of the stories by yourself. Your grandpa tells me you're a great reader. I'll be back when I go off duty, and we can read some of it today."

She was glad he was coming back. She wished he would spend more time in her room—she felt safe when he was there. Sometimes she wished Grandpa and Grandma would leave and just Dr. Alexander and Miss Whitaker would stay with her.

The cake must have been the surprise. Everyone left the room except her grandparents. Grandma set the leftover cake on the chest and fussed around with the bedspread. "Why don't I put a pair of your new pajamas on you?" she asked. "Which ones would you like?"

If she could shrug her shoulders, she would.

"These green ones are lovely," Grandma went on. Grandpa went to walk up and down the hall while Grandma got Christie into the pajamas. She brought the mirror for her to look at herself. Christie didn't even try to smile. Grandma was working so hard to please her, and Christie wished she wouldn't. The hospital gown, that white tent that tied in the back, was easier to put on and felt better too. She knew she was crabby, but who cared?

Grandma had taken off the sneakers to pull on the pajamas, then she forgot to put them back on. She just covered Christie's stockinged feet with the bedding, and then she did a surprising thing. She carried the sneakers to the closet, set them inside, and closed the door. Miss Whitaker wouldn't like it a bit when she found out, Christie thought.

Grandma raised the back of the bed, then went to fiddle with the new cards on the windowsill. She folded the old get-well greetings and put them in the top drawer of the chest. There must be hundreds of them by now. They had shown Christie all of them, including the letters from the kids at school and Sunday school, but most of the time she was too sleepy to pay much attention.

Grandpa stuck his head in the door. "Ready?" Then he added, "Are you decent?"

Once—it seemed a long time ago—that would have made her laugh. Would she ever laugh out loud again? She didn't even want to smile, and she didn't need to make a noise to do that. How could Grandpa joke? Didn't he care that Mom and Dad were dead? He and Grandma didn't even care that

Benjamin was thousands of miles away, that Rusty was staying at someone else's house.

Grandpa held the door open, and in ran Brenda, her blond ponytail swinging. She was grinning and her green eyes were snapping with pleasure. "Hi, Christie!" she said, very fast. "They let me in special today because it's your birthday." Her best friend stopped beside the bed, looked at Christie, and the grin disappeared. Tears welled up in her eyes. She brushed them away and talked even faster. "You'll love what I've got in this bag!"

Christie felt her own tears as they spilled over. Why was she crying? She thought she'd never been so glad to see anyone in her life. She couldn't talk, but she could let Brenda know how she felt. While the tears rolled down to her chin, she smiled.

Grandma was sniffling again and Grandpa was chuckling. Her grandmother went to the other side of the bed, wiped Christie's face with a tissue, then dabbed at her nose.

Laughing, Brenda wiped her eyes and blew her nose. She took a small calculator from the bag. "The class sent you this. We worked for it. We had slave days when we did jobs for people and they paid us. I dusted shelves of books in the back room at the library. Some kids washed windows, some shoveled snow. You name it, they did it!"

Christie noticed she was talking louder and louder, as if she thought her friend were deaf. Without asking permission, she stepped up onto the bottom rung of the bed rails that were lowered during the day and climbed up to plunk herself down beside Christie. Almost shouting, she said, "Our Sunday school class went hiking, and you won't believe all that's happened since you've been away from school."

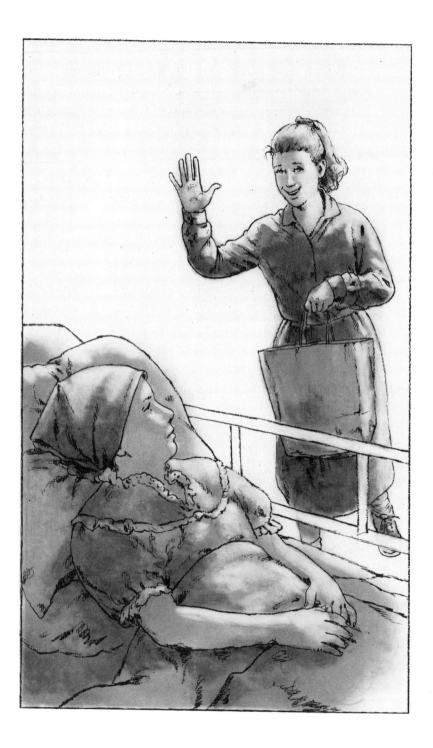

"Christie can't talk, Brenda, but she can hear fine." Grandpa said the words kindly, but Christie could see that her friend was embarrassed. She blinked fast and her cheeks got pink. "Sorry," she said in a normal voice. "I'm dumb sometimes."

Grandma cut a piece of birthday cake for Brenda and said, "Grandpa and I'll be back tonight. When she gets sleepy, you should leave, dear. Don't forget."

"I won't," Brenda promised. When they were gone, she said, "You want a bite?" She got two clean forks from the tray, climbed back onto the bed and took a bite, then popped another into Christie's mouth with the second fork. It was *good*. How come it was moist and tasty when Brenda gave it to her? She'd have to think about that.

"Rusty misses you. He sleeps in my room. He even sneaks up on the bed as soon as daylight comes. I think Mother knows, but she just sticks a sheet over my blanket and doesn't say anything. Can you believe that?" Brenda licked some blue frosting off the paper plate, then let it sail, like a Frisbee, toward the wastebasket. "Missed! I'll pick it up later."

The stupid tears had started again when Brenda mentioned Rusty. When Christie thought of the red and white dog, wagging madly every time any of his family came home no matter how long they'd been gone, the pit of her stomach ached. Rusty must think they'd given him away—that they didn't want him anymore. She knew she was jealous of Brenda because he might as well be her dog now. Christie closed her eyes. Dumb tears.

She felt Brenda wiping her face with a tissue, as Grandma had. "I thought you'd want to know he's doing okay."

Christie tried to smile at her, and Brenda chattered on about daily happenings at school. Christie didn't want to sleep because she didn't want the words to stop, but right in the middle of a sentence she dropped off, and when she woke up again, her friend was gone. Christie decided she must be practically a baby again. She couldn't talk, everyone had to take care of her, she slept all the time, and she couldn't feed herself. Worst of all, she couldn't even go to the bathroom by herself. They had to put her on one of those shiny, cold bedpans.

She had been thinking with her eyes closed, and now she felt the bed sink down on one side as if someone were pressing on it. She opened her eyes. Dr. Alexander was sitting beside her, right in the spot Brenda had left. He wasn't wearing his regular green doctor jacket; he wore blue jeans and a green sweat shirt with white letters that spelled DARTMOUTH.

"You've had a big day," he said. "I promised I'd read some of the story of Rip Van Winkle. Think you can keep those gorgeous eyes open for a while?"

She looked at him, trying to make her eyes tell him how glad she was to see him, trying to tell him she was interested in hearing him read the story.

He opened the book and began. His wonderful voice, the rhythm of the words, and the pictures in her mind took her away from the pink room to the Catskill Mountains, then along the Hudson River. The story wasn't like the ones that talked to kids as if they were too dumb to understand. These words pleased her, and Dr. Alexander knew just how to say them. When he read that Rip Van Winkle was a henpecked husband, she knew he was just like Grandpa, and her mind turned him into "Theodore." The way Rip played with the children and knew how to make toys for them and tell them stories—that *was* Grandpa. Wouldn't Grandma be surprised if Christie called her Dame MacLane? Rip Van Winkle would rather fish than work, and he loved to hunt in the woods. Washington Irving must have known Grandpa!

Dr. Alexander read the whole story, and Christie stayed awake, watching his face. It was very tanned, as if he'd been at the beach all summer, even though it was just April. He was about Dad's age and had brown eyes, too. His brown hair was short and straight, not wavy like Dad's. His nose was a little long, but very straight, and she could see his shiny white teeth while he read. When he stood up, he was very tall, and he walked in sort of a springy way, as if he had on thick rubber soles.

Now she knew why he called her Miss Van Winkle. Old Rip had slept for twenty years and she had slept for weeks and weeks, but just as Rip Van Winkle said in the story, it seemed like one night. When she woke up, everything had been changed for her too.

The doctor put the book on her table. "It was great to read that again. How'd you like it?"

She smiled.

After Christie was fed, Grandpa and Grandma came back, and Grandpa said, "One more surprise. Think you can stand it, sweetie?" Christie tried to picture him with a long, white beard.

She was interested and she didn't feel crabby. She wasn't bored or sleepy. What was the surprise?

When the telephone on the table buzzed, Grandpa lifted it from its cradle. "Hello!" he said. "How's the big boy?" He grinned at Christie. "It's Benjamin." She opened her eyes wide as Grandpa spoke into the phone again. "She won't be able to talk, but she can hear your voice." Then he held the phone against her ear.

"Christie! It's Benjamin! I miss you and I want to come home. Can you hear me?" Tears slid down Christie's face. She couldn't speak, but she had to do something to let him know she was there. He spoke again. "Happy birthday, Christie. . . . Christie?"

She puckered her lips and strained to make a sound. Her lips parted, and she sent a loud smacking noise to Benjamin, way out in California.

Grandpa and Grandma took turns talking to Benjamin, then to Aunt Harriet and Uncle Will.

Christie held the sound of her brother's voice in her head. She closed her eyes and saw the rusty-haired, sturdy eight-year-old who had freckles all over his short nose and cheeks. His shining brown eyes were always darting here and there, "looking for some trouble to get into," Mom had often said. In her mind's picture, Rusty was there too, his fur the color of Benjamin's hair. His tail wagged and he leaned against his boy.

3

Second Most Important

Days came and went, and Christie couldn't tell one from the other. She had plenty of time to think. Even when someone was in the room, she often closed her eyes and tried to make it seem real that Mom and Dad were dead. She told herself it was true, but sometimes she expected them to be there when she woke up. No one had ever said the word *dead* when they talked to her the day she'd dreamed about the accident.

Maybe they were away somewhere, in some other hospital, getting well. Then why did Grandpa and Grandma stay here all the time? Why did that aching feeling in the pit of her stomach keep coming back? And Grandma cried so much. Grandpa's violet eyes—they must be just like her own—had a deep sadness in them that she had never seen before. They looked sad even when he made his funny little remarks to her. She was so confused. But would anyone tell her anything, even if she could ask questions?

Dr. Alexander could make her forget for a while. A few days after Benjamin called, he came to sit with her. He wore his DARTMOUTH sweat shirt and his blue jeans. He was like two different people: one, the doctor who kept her safe; the other, a friend who talked and read to her. When he read "The Legend of Sleepy Hollow," her eyes glowed, she was sure; and they must get big in the spooky parts. He read it in three afternoons.

The next time he came before supper. He sat on the bed and looked at her. "Miss Van Winkle, Ellen tells me you aren't trying. She can't do it all, you know. You have to make an effort to move those muscles yourself. She says you just lie there like a blob of jelly. Why is that? I should think you'd want to pick up that book and read it. How do you think your class would feel if they could see that calculator over there on the chest, just going to waste? Your grandparents come in here every day, hoping you'll move a finger or a toe. We'll never know how much you can do if you don't try."

Christie felt the ever-ready tears fill her eyes. How did he expect her to move when nothing worked right? It wasn't her fault, was it? She had thought he understood.

Dr. Alexander didn't seem to see the tears. "I want you to do something for me. It'll be our secret. Whenever you're alone, look down at your right foot and say to your big toe, *'I'm going to move you, you lazy slob.'*"

She glared at the black sneakers.

Dr. Alexander said, "Okay, you're right. How can you see if the lazy slob moves in those things? I'll tell Miss Whitaker you can shed those when your company leaves. I want you to wear them at night, but when you're by yourself, you start giving that big toe the old mean eye."

For him, she'd do it, even though she knew her toe would never move. Besides, she liked to play games.

Like a mind reader, Dr. Alexander said, "This isn't a game, Miss Van Winkle. It's the second most important thing in your life right now." He didn't explain. She tried to plead with her eyes, but he stood up and said, "I'll see you in the morning." He kissed his finger, then pressed it against the end of her nose. He left without telling her what the first most important thing was.

After Grandma fed her from the tray on the stand and let her drink milk from the bent straw, Grandpa unlaced the sneakers. He slipped them off and pulled off the white knee socks, then he folded the bedding over her ankles so she could see her feet sticking up. "This little pig went to market," he said and tweaked her little toe. He had done that when she was a little kid. "Dr. Alexander was very mysterious about all this. Wish you could tell me what's going on, sweetie."

Dr. Alexander did understand, after all. It was their secret.

At first it seemed important to look right at her big toe and think, *I'm going to move you, you lazy slob.* She glared at her toe until her eyes burned and she felt sweaty. But nothing happened. Nothing at all. She was glad when the nurse came in to put the sneakers back on. She wouldn't have to look at that hateful toe another minute.

The next morning when Dr. Alexander came in, Miss Whitaker was with him. He didn't mention their secret. He sent the nurse on an errand and asked, "How did it go, Miss Van Winkle?"

She was so angry, her eyes must be snapping. "Just what I thought," he said. "You expected that lazy slob to move the very first day, didn't you? It might be a long time before you get that toe to move. I'm betting you can be patient and show him who's boss." He pulled off the sneakers and socks and set them in a chair. "Might as well start now, while you wait for your grandparents to come."

I'm going to move you, you lazy slob. I'm going to move you, you lazy slob. She concentrated on the big toe, but it ignored her. This morning she didn't feel so angry. When Grandma put the socks and sneakers back on, Christie wasn't even annoyed.

Grandpa brought in a big tablet of white paper. "I'm sick of sitting here with nothing to do. I've thought up something that will keep me entertained." He pressed the button that raised the back of the bed until she was in a half-sitting position. He sat on the edge of the bed and wrote a word at the top of the first sheet of paper. *Colors.*

"Can you read that okay?"

Although the soft, padded collar they kept around her neck and the tubelike pillow kept her head from rolling to the sides, she could see a wide area of the room. Of course she could see that word. He was holding it up in front of her.

First he wrote *red,* using a ball-point pen. "Can you find anything this color around here?"

There was a red flower in a bouquet on the chest, and a red pencil beside the menu list on a small table. There was a get-well card on the windowsill, and Grandma's cheeks had two round spots of red where she rubbed on her rouge from the little round box in her purse. Her lips were bright red today too. Christie thought she had found all the reds, then she spotted red lines in the plaid design on Grandma's blouse.

She looked at Grandpa.

"So, you've found all of them, heh? Make it tough, now. Pick one for me to find and see how sharp I can be."

She decided on Grandma's cheeks. He'd never think of that!

It took Grandpa a long time to touch each red thing in the room and then turn to Christie. She had to keep her eyes open for no and closed for yes.

Grandpa was smart all right. He found two things she had missed: red letters on a sign on the inside of the door, and red speckles in his button-up sweater. He never did notice Grandma's cheeks, though. Christie had to stare at Grandma until he caught on.

"That's one for you," he said, and he made a capital *C* beside the word *red*.

Next he wrote *blue*. There were fewer blues: the gloomy curtains, the matching plastic chairs, and a picture on the wall. Grandpa's eyes were blue, violet blue, but he couldn't see those.

She chose the picture on the wall, with its bright blue sky. Grandpa pointed to it right away and laughed, proud of himself. Christie knew how much he loved to win games. He never let Benjamin or her win at checkers or Monopoly just because they were kids. They had to work to win.

After he made a capital *T* for Theodore, he wrote *mauve* under *blue*.

What in the universe was that? She looked at the word, then at Grandpa.

"Sorry, kiddo. You have to find it yourself. I'll tell you one thing. It really *is* a color."

Yellow, green, pink; orange, brown, white; red and blue, Christie thought. What was different? It had to be a color that wasn't a common one, didn't it? Grandpa couldn't sit still on the bed, he was so gleeful. He stood up and paced back and forth, chuckling out loud.

"That's not fair, Theodore. The child doesn't know what mauve is." Grandma had come over to look at the paper and she clucked her tongue.

"No, but she knows what all the other colors are. She can use her common sense and find the one that isn't just a plain old color, right?"

"I think you're mean!" insisted Grandma.

"Don't you dare tell her!" He grinned at Christie. "Think you've found anything mauve?" Grandpa was so sure she didn't know, Christie was determined to find that color.

"Give up?"

She didn't. He sat down in the blue chair and watched her, still grinning.

She began to feel grumpy. Mauve! The word even sounded ugly. It must be a smelly color!

Just then, she noticed her arm on the white bedspread. Her pajama sleeve was a pale shade of lavender, certainly not an ordinary color. Was that what he meant by mauve? If she could find something else that shade, she'd have two he might have chosen. She studied everything she could see.

Grandma's silver hair wasn't really silver; it was a pale lavender, too, a special tint the hairdresser put in the rinse every Friday afternoon. Christie had Grandpa this time! But she had picked Grandma's rouge before. She picked the pajamas. He went right to Grandma and patted her soft hair. "Got you!"

Christie kept her eyes wide open. Grandpa looked funny, as if he couldn't believe what had happened. He looked around for some time, then shrugged. "You've got me." He wasn't smiling.

When Christie looked down at her sleeve, he said, "Oh, no! Right under my nose."

The capital *C* beside *mauve* gave her a two-out-of-three win, and Grandpa drew a line under the three words to mark the end of the game. "Would you believe it? It's almost time for your lunch," he said.

The morning had sailed by. They heard the dishes clinking on the cart in the hall, and Christie could smell beef in the air. Grandma rolled the tray stand over the bed and washed Christie's hands. For once, she felt hungry.

Daytimes went by faster now. Christie tried to concentrate on Ellen's directions when she came in for exercise therapy. Dr. Alexander said he was pleased with Ellen's report of her improved attitude. She hadn't noticed any difference in herself. She didn't talk and she didn't move. Maybe she wasn't trying hard enough.

I'm going to move you, you lazy slob. Christie thought that sentence many times a day, even when her sneakers were on and someone was in the room. She stared at her right big toe and tried to force it to move. She'd know if it happened inside the sneaker.

Grandpa invented more games for the pad of paper. One day he wrote a list of vegetables and numbered them. He made up silly stories, and Christie tried to guess which vegetable was the star of each. She blinked her eyes to show the number beside the vegetable's name. Grandpa included *endive* on the list and, as she had with *mauve,* she used her common sense to help decide which story described the unfamiliar food.

Grandpa always managed to stick in some word she'd never heard before.

Another time, he numbered a list of names, including Benjamin, Rusty, Brenda, Grandma's first name, Elizabeth, people from books she had read, and characters from history. He told situations in which each one had taken part. Christie had to connect the stories to the right names. Grandpa insisted he was doing this to keep himself awake.

While they played, Grandma worked on sewing an outfit for Christie. She'd have liked to make a pink, ruffly, fluffy dress, Christie knew, but she didn't. She sewed tiny gold butterfly buttons on the green blouse and she stitched a gold butterfly on the pocket. Grandma must be looking ahead to the time when Christie would be out of bed. She wasn't making pajamas or a bathrobe or knitting slipper socks; she was making something for Christie to wear when she got up! She began to hope.

Her hair was growing, and Grandpa held the mirror for her to watch while Grandma brushed the short stuff.

Brenda came every Sunday afternoon. Dr. Alexander had given permission for her to be admitted in spite of the rule that no one under fourteen could come in. He called it treatment, weekend therapy, and special medicine. How could the bosses say no to something so healing?

Often Christie thought about Benjamin and wished she could call him for a surprise. Brenda gave her news about Rusty, but she wanted to pat his red fur and hug him around his neck. She wouldn't even mind if he slobbered all over her with one of his kisses.

During the day it was easy to keep herself from thinking about Mom and Dad, but when the nurse turned off her light, the ache in the pit of her stomach came back. It helped to talk to them, to tell them she was sorry about being angry. She talked to God too. He could have stopped the accident, couldn't He? Why had He let this happen to her? Sometimes she felt guilty. In a way, it was all her fault—she had begged and begged to go to the mall that day.

Sometimes she cried herself to sleep, and sometimes she woke herself up trying to scream, "Mom! Dad! We need you. Come home!"

4

A Letter from Benjamin

"It's time you were aware of what day it is," Grandpa said. He taped a poster-sized calendar to the wall, right in front of Christie's bed. The black numbers were huge, and the illustration above the squares showed a girl riding a bicycle along a country road that was bordered on both sides by a forest. A rusty-colored dog trotted along behind her on the gravelly road.

Grandpa drew crosses through the first ten numbers with a felt-tipped, black-capped pen. Then he lifted a red-capped pen from his shirt pocket.

"This one's for our red-letter days, sweetie. I think this calendar tells the future in more than days. That's Christie in the picture and the dog is Rusty. When you feel discouraged, you just look at that, put yourself on that bicycle, and pedal away."

I love you, Grandpa, she thought, and she tried to put that feeling into her eyes when she looked at his. He bent down and kissed her cheek. He knew.

JUNE

Monday	Tuesday	Wednesday	Thursday	Friday	Saturday
		1	2	3	4
6	7	8	9	10	11

He walked over to look out the window; Grandma was standing there, watering a pink-flowered plant that Christie's Sunday school class had sent. Grandma spoke in a whisper, but Christie heard what she said. "Sometimes I think you're heartless. How do you think she'll feel, looking at that picture every day while she has to lie like a rock in her bed?"

Grandpa made a hushing sound, but Grandma whispered on. "She has to face the truth, Theodore. Don't put dreams into her head."

Then Grandpa spoke out loud. "There are no impossible dreams, Elizabeth. And God still does miracles."

Grandma sighed.

When they left, Christie looked at the picture. The girl on the bicycle wore a green shirt and blue jeans, and the dog had a bright green collar. The trees arched over the road, turning it into a tunnel. The shaded surface was speckled with spots of sunshine. In the distance, the road led to bright sunlight, and Christie was heading right toward it. The name seemed natural for the girl.

I'm going to move you, you lazy slob, she thought, and she glared at her bare big toe. Nothing. *I'm going to move you, you lazy slob.* Still nothing. Dr. Alexander believed she could be patient. He had said she'd move that toe, hadn't he? *I'm going to move you, you lazy slob.* Nothing.

A volunteer lady in her blue smock came in while Christie was concentrating on the stubborn toe. "A letter for you, young lady, and some more cards. You're such a popular girl."

Christie watched her put the envelopes on the tray stand. Mrs. Doyle was as old as Grandma, but her silver hair was really silver. She was short and plump, while Grandma was tall and thin. She looked at Christie. "Can you wait, or do you want me to read that letter to you? Your grandparents will be back soon, won't they? In case you're interested, it's from California, and it looks like a little kid's handwriting."

Benjamin! She didn't want to wait. She looked at the volunteer hopefully. Mrs. Doyle sat on the edge of the bed and lifted the flap of the envelope. First she looked at the back and found the name. "Benjamin wrote this. Do you know who Benjamin is? What a silly question. Of course you do, or he wouldn't be writing, would he?" She laughed.

Christie wanted to grab the letter and read it herself. Why was that woman talking so much?

At last Mrs. Doyle read, and she made no more comments.

> Dear Christie,
>
> When can I come home? I think I'm alurjick. Sometime I weez in bed and Jeff and Allan are mad because they cant sleep. Then Aunt Harryet puts me out on the liveing room sofer for the rest of the night.
>
> When are you going to be better? Sally says they can get rid of me when you are all well. Cusins arnt so nice. Jeff thinks my cot is a bum deal in his room.
>
> Its hot out here and school is boyling. Debra is my age, so I'm stuck with her most evry day. Shes nex door. Bill is 16 and drives Uncel Wills car. Marnies nice. Shes 12 like you.
>
> When Im alurjick sometime I dream about Mum and Dad. They want me and you and Rusty to come home.
>
> Love,
>
> Benjamin

The deep pain in the pit of her stomach had started almost as soon as Mrs. Doyle began to read. She hadn't looked at Christie while she read, so she hadn't noticed that she was crying. When Mrs. Doyle held the letter close for her to see, the big writing and the funny mistakes dragged a quivery sob from Christie's mouth, and her chest heaved as she sucked in gulps of air.

Mrs. Doyle looked startled, and her eyes filled. "Oh, dear. I shouldn't have read that to you—now you're upset. I should have waited for your grandparents to come back."

She folded the letter and set it on the stand, took a small tissue from the box on the table, and wiped Christie's eyes and nose. "I'm sorry. Don't cry anymore, please." She went out and left the door open behind her.

Almost immediately, Miss Whitaker came in.

The nurse bustled around, turned Christie over, and rubbed her back. It didn't stop the pain, and Christie couldn't stop crying. Although the bedding didn't need to be straightened, Miss Whitaker did it anyway. "Mrs. Doyle said you had a letter from your brother and that he was homesick," she said softly. "It's natural for him to feel like that every once in a while, Christie. If the truth were known, he's probably enjoying himself most of the time. Who wouldn't, in California? They've got Disneyland, beautiful mountains, and the Pacific Ocean beaches out there. He's a lucky boy, you know."

If it was such fun, his letter would say so, wouldn't it? Christie's crying had turned into hiccupping noises, and her eyelids felt heavy and swollen.

Dr. Alexander burst into the room. "Taxi! Did someone in here call a taxi?" He pushed a reclining, padded chair on wheels, steering it to the bedside. "The grand tour begins in five minutes. Is my passenger ready?" He wore his DART-MOUTH sweat shirt and jeans, and he held out a smaller copy of the sweat shirt. He worked it over Christie's head and onto her arms, then he held her up while he pulled the green waistband down over her stomach. It was loose and baggy, just the way she liked her shirts.

"There! You're all ready to travel. Please get a blanket out of the closet, Miss Whitaker. Lap robes are in style here."

He never mentioned her swollen eyes or her nose that must be red. He tucked the blanket around her hips and wrapped her legs and feet. The sneakers were on the chair, and he left them there.

She had imagined what the corridor looked like; now she would see the real thing. From where they started, she could see the length of the hall because her room was second from the end on the right. Some of the doors were propped open, and a few people in bathrobes walked slowly down the hall, holding onto wall railings.

"Hi, Christie." A red-haired woman in a bright pink robe knew who she was.

A red-faced man who looked very fat in his blue robe, said, "Hello there, neighbor. Glad to see you out for a ride."

"Meet Jack Rosen, Christie," the doctor said. "Are you behaving yourself, Jack?"

Mr. Rosen grinned at Christie. "That's no fun, is it, Christie? Plenty of time for behaving when we go home," he said. "Lucky you've got Doc taking care of you."

She thought so too.

They passed a young woman wearing a white silk robe who walked in slow motion, holding one hand on her stomach as if she were afraid it might fall off if she let go.

"You're so pretty," she told Christie. "When I get out of here, I'm getting a haircut just like yours. It's so smart and just right for the hot days. Those are neat sweat shirts."

Christie tried to smile.

The nurses' desk wasn't a desk at all; it was a long counter with nurses behind it, like clerks in a store. They all noticed Christie on the rolling recliner. "Hi! It's about time you got down here to see us. How about getting all of us sweat shirts like that, Dr. Alexander?" one of them asked.

He pushed the recliner right behind the desk, and she could see long shelves under the counter. There was a telephone and metal-covered binders that must be full of information about the patients. Christie had seen one in the doctor's hands when he talked to Miss Whitaker in her room. On the shelves were pens, pencils, plastic coffee cups, and tiny measuring containers with colored pills and capsules, along with things Christie didn't recognize. Dr. Alexander rolled the recliner out again.

They crossed the hall to an alcove where four elevators stood. The doors of the farther one on the left glided open, and Grandpa and Grandma stepped out, looking surprised.

"Look who's here to greet us." Grandpa jumped back, pretending to be shocked. Grandma kissed Christie's head.

"Our tour is half over," Dr. Alexander told them.

"We'll be in the room, sweetie," said Grandpa.

Through swinging doors that opened automatically when they got near them, her taxi moved along to the other end of the corridor. They entered a large room furnished with plastic-covered chairs of yellow, orange, and brown. There was an orange sofa that could probably hold three or four people. Christie's attention flew to a giant television set with the widest screen she had ever seen.

"That interests you, doesn't it?" Dr. Alexander asked. "We'll see what we can do about having Grandpa toot you down here once in a while. Would you like that?"

Would I like that! she thought. It doesn't matter what show is on; I'll watch everything.

Back in the hall, the doctor stopped the recliner near the wall and walked around to where Christie could see him. "A TV set can be rented for your room, but I've advised against that for now. I don't want you to spend your days looking at shows, or your second most important job in the world will be neglected. One hour each day your grandparents can bring you down here to watch the big set. Think you and they can figure out which time you'd like best?"

Her eyes felt better, and she could imagine that they were sparkling right now.

"I want you to meet someone." He wheeled the recliner to the end of the hall and out onto a glassed-in porch. Near a window was a young man, maybe eighteen years old, and he lay on a recliner like hers.

"This is Jonathan Peters, Christie." Dr. Alexander sat down on the flowered cushion of a white wicker chair. Christie and Jonathan looked at each other.

"Hi, Chri—tie." Jonathan spoke slowly, leaving out the "s" sound. She could tell that talking was hard for him. "Great day." He reached his hand toward her in greeting. His wrist was bent and his thumb drawn back toward his arm.

Why didn't Dr. Alexander say something? Christie looked at him.

But it was Jonathan who spoke. "Van Wink—kle." Then, slowly and loudly, "Ha! Ha!" His laugh reminded her of the way a cassette player sounds when its batteries are low. He went on, "Me too."

She understood. Jonathan had been in a coma. But now he was talking and he could move his hand. His long fingers held a paperback book open in his lap.

His brown eyes smiled. She didn't know whether Jonathan was tall or short, but he was very thin. His hair was clipped and stubbly, and it was a very dark brown, almost black. His nose was a little crooked and a red scar ran down from the bridge across his right cheek. Along each side of the scar were red dots—stitch marks, she thought.

As if he could hear her questions, Jonathan said, "Ack—dent. Car. Too fat. Dumb me."

For sure, he wasn't too fat. What did he mean? It didn't take her long to figure out he meant "fast."

Dr. Alexander stood up. "You two guys don't have to say it all now. Christie's company is waiting, and she's had a big day for her first trip."

"Vit?" Jonathan asked. Christie couldn't figure it out. He tried again. "Me. Vit you?"

Visit! She'd have to remember he left out his "s" sounds.

"To—mor—row." Jonathan lifted his bent hand and waved it at her.

The doctor pushed the recliner directly to room 310. When he lifted her onto the bed and pulled off the sweat shirt, Christie was actually glad to feel the familiar mattress and sheet under her. Grandma tucked the bedding under her chin, and Dr. Alexander motioned to her grandparents to follow him out to the corridor. She felt herself drifting off to sleep while she waited for them to come back.

5

Red-Letter Day

By keeping her eyes closed, Christie heard more than anyone realized. Several times she had heard her grandparents praying over her, asking God to help her get well. Grandpa always ended by saying, "No matter what happens, Lord, let her see that You love her."

Sometimes she heard things not meant for her ears. Grandpa and Grandma whispered, thinking she was asleep, but she could hear. That's how she knew Grandma had called their son, Uncle Will, and told him to be sure he and Aunt Harriet checked all the letters that Benjamin wrote in the future. They didn't want Christie upset. It was Grandma's idea, but Grandpa didn't argue.

In the same way, she learned that they had rented out Christie and Benjamin's family house in Wilson. Would some other girl use her furniture, her games and dolls, her bicycle? Perhaps someone would read her journal, her private thoughts. What about Benjamin's bunk beds, his collection of miniature road equipment, and his cars? Would they get rid of Rusty's beds, one in the living room and one in Benjamin's bedroom? It was a strain to keep her eyes from flying open with panic.

After one nap, Christie heard Grandma talking about a trust fund they would set up in the Sharpe Commercial Bank for their college. Christie didn't know what a trust fund was, but she knew from the conversation that the house would be sold and the money put into the trust fund.

Christie's routine had changed since Dr. Alexander took her on that first tour. Every day, Grandpa rolled her recliner down to the television room. She made the choices while Grandpa read out the TV listings. Game shows were her favorite.

The day after she met Jonathan Peters, he came to visit. Miss Whitaker wheeled his recliner in and placed it beside her bed so they could look at each other.

"You can mile, Chri—tie," he said in his slow way.

She wanted to laugh. There was something funny about hearing a grown-up fellow like him talking that way. She struggled to keep her lips from twitching.

"Mile take mull," Jonathan told her.

What was mull? She had no idea.

He tried again. "Mile take mull." This time, he bent his arm and felt the muscle in the upper part, like Popeye.

Smiles take muscles! He was right. It did take muscles to smile.

"You can talk, Chri—tie."

He wasn't making sense. If she could talk, she'd be doing it, wouldn't she?

"Mile," he said.

She stretched her mouth.

"Good. Keep miling. Go m-m-m-m-m."

Christie held the smile. "M-m-m-m-m."

That wasn't talking; it was moaning.

"Keep it up. Keep it up. Open lip, keep it up."

She stretched the m-m-m-m-m sound and kept smiling, then opened her lips a bit. Just as clearly as anyone could say it, she said, "M-m-m-m-me."

"You talk, Chri—tie!"

She had to keep doing it, over and over again. She smiled, made the m-m-m-m-m sound, parted her lips, and out came "me." The more she did it, the better it was.

Jonathan slapped his palm against the back of the bent hand. "Ha! Ha! Ha! You talk!"

How dumb could she be? Her eyes filled with tears.

Grandpa and Grandma came in just then, introduced themselves to Jonathan, and kissed Christie. The two new friends looked at each other. Neither gave away Christie's news. She wanted to wait for the right time.

It finally came when Grandpa asked, "I wonder who'd like some of Grandma's special lemonade?" He patted a picnic jug he had set on the chest.

Jonathan's eyes laughed. "Me," he said.

Like a parrot, she said, "Me."

"Who?" Grandpa dropped the plastic cups.

Grandma whirled around from her daily puttering at the windowsill. "Christie!"

"Me! Me! Me!" She grinned.

Grandpa lifted her right up in his arms. "You beautiful girl! You beautiful, beautiful girl! Oh, God is so good!"

Even at a time like this, Grandma said, "Careful, Theodore." She laughed at herself and hugged them both.

Jonathan laughed his slow "Ha! Ha! Ha!"

Grandpa wasted no time in spreading the news to the nurses, and they informed Dr. Alexander. Again, the room filled with the floor nurses, the doctor, Mr. Rosen, and even a lady patient Christie had never seen before. Like a performer, she said "Me" for each one.

After a few minutes, Dr. Alexander shooed everybody out, allowing only her grandparents, Miss Whitaker, and Jonathan to stay. "Tell me all about it," he demanded.

Grandma thought she had it straight. "She just said it when Theodore asked if anyone would like some of my lemonade."

Christie had to let them know that Jonathan had been the one to show her that she could talk. If she could say *me,* maybe she could say a rhyming word.

She smiled, parted her lips, forced out a long breath, and said, "He." Christie looked directly at Jonathan.

Everyone understood.

Dr. Alexander said, "What happened, Jonathan?"

"Chri—tie mile. Make m-m-m-m and open lip."

It was Grandpa who caught on first. "You told her how to do that, didn't you?"

Jonathan's face was red. "Yea."

Grandpa pumped his hand up and down, the one that was bent at the wrist.

Jonathan looked embarrassed.

Grandma kissed his cheek and said, "We can never thank you enough for this."

Poor Jonathan, Christie thought. Too bad he had to take all that gushing and smooching, but she'd had to let them know that it was his idea.

When Miss Whitaker wheeled Jonathan's recliner to the door, he waved his hand at Christie. "To—mor—row," he said.

She was glad he'd be back.

"See you in a few minutes, Jonathan," Dr. Alexander called after him.

Christie had almost forgotten about that lazy slob of a toe in the excitement of discovering that she could speak. "Never mind that toe. If I can say two words, I can say more," she told herself.

It always seemed that the doctor could read her mind. "Try all you want, Miss Van Winkle. Who knows what you can do? You're my miracle girl." He left, turning back at the door to blow her a kiss.

With the red felt-tipped pen, Grandpa circled June second on the calendar. "Yes," he said. "A miracle girl. That's a wonderful thing God did for you, sweetie. He loves you very much, you know."

She didn't want to think about that, so she didn't look at him. She kept her eyes on the calendar. In May, the eleventh had been the first red-letter day, for her first ride outside room 310. Although they didn't know, she also remembered it as the day Benjamin's letter had come. She couldn't forget his unhappy question, "When can I come home?" Someday she'd answer.

Grandma thought that Christie would forget all about it, because she had tucked the letter away in the drawer with the pile of cards. She never would. Dad used to say, "This family sticks together." It was up to her to make sure of that.

"Me. He." Christie repeated the words many times and Grandpa wrote them down on his pad of paper.

"You talk, and I'll keep a list. I'll bet it will be a long one."

He wrote *me* and *he*. "All set when you are. I'm the secretary."

"Don't push her, Theodore," Grandma warned. She didn't look up from the raspberry-colored sweater she was knitting for Christie. Already, she had finished a button-up, cocoa-colored one for Benjamin. She said the nights were cool in California.

Grandpa was waiting. There was no rhyming word she couldn't say, she felt sure. Maybe going alphabetically would be fun.

Christie pressed her lips together and smiled. Her cheeks puffed out and she let the air explode as she tried to hold the smile in place. She was gritting her teeth too hard. When she managed to relax them, it was easier, and she said, "Be." She said it three times before it sounded right to her. Grandpa wrote it under *he*.

Fee was simple. She smiled and blew through her lips, then she parted them, and there it was, "Fee."

No matter how hard she worked, when she tried to say "gee," all she produced was "chee."

"Never mind, sweetie," Grandpa said, "at least we know you can make the 'ch' sound." Even though it wasn't a real word, he wrote *chee* in the next space.

As she said "key," she realized she hadn't even thought about how to make the "k" sound; it just popped out, naturally.

She had to smile with her mouth open to get her tongue up behind her top teeth to say "Lee." Grandpa wrote it with a small "l," but she thought of it with a capital. Lee Barry was a boy in the sixth grade at Wilson Elementary. Brenda drooled over him.

"We'd better stop after this one so you can decide what show you want to watch today," Grandpa said. Grandma must have been sending him eyebrow signals.

"Knee." Again, she had to start with an open smile. Funny, she'd never noticed what a big deal words were for her tongue, her lips, and her breath. She had to press her tongue behind her upper teeth again to make the "n" sound, almost as she had with the "l." And those sounds weren't even alike.

After Grandpa wrote *knee,* he counted. "Seven words, the 'ch' sound and all in one day. Oops, I forgot the 'ee' sound."

He drew his bushy eyebrows down like he did whenever he was getting ready to say something serious. "You're doing great, sweetie. But listen, no matter what you can do or can't do, remember that God loves you."

Yes, she told him with her eyes, she tried to remember.

"You belong to Him," Grandpa went on, "and He cares about what happens to you—even though it's hard to understand right now."

Grandpa smiled at her, and she tried to smile back. Then Grandma put away the knitting and readied Christie for her lunch. She was hungry enough to eat a hippopotamus.

6

A Door Unlocked

Christie was relieved to find that she could say the "s" sound. She had worried that she'd have the same difficulty Jonathan had. Words came fast after the first day she spoke, and it seemed as though she'd been let out of a dark room after someone had locked her in.

She thought whole words in her head, but they came out in beginnings. "Gram" was her name for both grandparents, "Bren," "Jon," and "Doc Al" were her friends' names. Besides that, she left out parts of sentences.

Every day Jonathan visited, and they talked about what he planned to do when he could walk again and get back to Keene State College.

"Geh what I'm going to tudy." He had waited for Christie to answer.

Now that she talked like a baby, Christie didn't feel like laughing at Jonathan's speech. "Doc? Law? Fire? Act? Art?"

Jonathan shook his head after each guess.

"I give up. Tell me."

"A peech ther—a—pit," he told her. She thought this was one of his jokes, so she laughed.

"I mean it," he said.

"How can you be a spee ther?" She thought about Miss Holland at Wilson Elementary, who came to her class twice a week to take Oscar Snow to the nurse's office for a lesson. He stuttered, and everyone called him one of the "special kids." After a minute she asked, "Is that what you stud in col?"

"No, I tudy com—pu—ter. Don't wor—ry, Chri—tie. I learn from peech ther—a—pit right here, and one day I'll be per—fect when I talk."

Christie believed him.

When Dr. Alexander made his extra visits, she knew he planned a mystery ride whenever he took out her DART-MOUTH sweat shirt, slipped it over her head, and settled her onto the recliner. So far, her favorite trip had been to the nursery. He had rolled the recliner up to the huge window, and from there she watched the nine babies. The boys were wrapped in blue blankets and the girls in pink. Some were sleeping, others stared at the ceiling, and two were howling. With all that racket, she wondered how the others could sleep.

They laughed when they counted three bald heads, all on girls! The nurses had tied pink bows on little spears of hair that stuck up on the other two girls. One boy had black hair so thick that Christie said, "It looks like a wig."

A tiny red-haired baby girl, dressed in only diapers, lay in a glass box. "That incubator keeps Judie warm and free from germs while she's growing big enough to go home," the doctor told Christie. "She's a fighter, just like you."

Christie felt very close to the small baby.

While they watched, a nurse with a mask over her mouth reached into the holes in the sides of the glass and gently cradled the baby in her hands. She's so helpless, Christie thought. Just like me.

When she had started to talk again, she expected to quickly be able to move her hands, her legs, and her feet. She had concentrated on her toe, and she had tried hard when Ellen worked with her on therapy days. *I'm going to move you, you lazy slob*, echoed through her dreams, but her toe didn't move.

Days passed—all the same—and one morning during Dr. Alexander's visit, she cried.

"What's the matter, Miss Van Winkle?"

"I nev walk or move hands, am I?" She said it as a question, but she felt that she was telling a fact. Why was he kidding her, letting her think that stupid game she played with her big toe really meant something?

"I believe you will, Christie. You believe and keep trying. You're talking, aren't you? Remember—moving and talking are both the second most important things in your life right now."

"When you tell me first?" She knew she was pouting, and she felt grouchy. She wanted to bang her fists on the bed and kick her heels up and down.

"It's all right to be mad. Who wouldn't be?" Dr. Alexander grinned at her, then he added, "When the time is right, I'll tell you what the most important thing is."

Christie closed her eyes. When she slept, she dreamed she was as normal as she had been before the accident changed everything. Besides, she had learned that pretending to sleep was a good way to get away from there. Everyone left her alone, and she could listen or drift into real sleep, whichever she chose to do. When she woke up, she might not be so crabby.

On Sundays, Grandpa and Grandma didn't come to see her. They drove home, to Sharpe, to take care of stuff that had to be done. They went to church too. She'd received cards from people there that she didn't know, and one time Grandpa had said that the whole church was praying for her.

Christie had always loved to visit Grandma and Grandpa's house and sleep in her mother's old room. Grandma had left many of Mom's kid things there—pictures on the wall, books on the shelves, even the old-fashioned record player. Christie liked to wind up the machine tightly with a crank handle and play thick, old-fashioned records on it.

She knew that would be her room when she went "home." She wondered how she'd feel when she saw all those reminders of Mom. Just thinking about them started up the deep pain in her stomach. Then she relaxed. As long as she couldn't walk or move her hands, she wouldn't have to face that yet.

Brenda came every Sunday afternoon. Once she arrived, there was no time for sad memories and angry feelings. Even when Christie had been well, she could hardly keep up with Brenda's ideas and her long legs. As often as not, Brenda hooked her arm through Christie's when they walked, and Christie had to skip in a few extra steps to come out even. Here it was the same, only Brenda could roll the recliner around at her own speed and keep Christie involved in whatever she planned.

At first, Christie had been ashamed to let Brenda hear her mixed-up speech, but her friend didn't laugh at her. She beat her hands on the tray stand and jumped up in the air, hitting her heels together, a trick she had practiced a million times a day, back in the fourth grade.

Brenda chattered even faster than she moved, and they talked about Rusty, and about Christie's week, and about what happened during Brenda's latest adventure. She always filled her in on the news from their Sunday school class too. Christie remembered how the class used to pray for sick kids, and she guessed that they were probably praying for her. With all these people praying for her, would it make any difference to God? Did He even care that she couldn't move her big toe yet? She put the thought away for another time, when Brenda wasn't here.

After a nurse put Christie onto the recliner, Brenda usually pushed it to the television room, or to the porch where they could watch the visitors coming up the front walk. Sometimes Jonathan was there, and the three of them laughed a lot.

Today Brenda had come with two presents. One was a tall homemade card from their Sunday school class. It had a funny purple elephant on the front and inside it said MISSING YOU—TONS. All the kids had signed it. Down at the bottom someone had printed a Bible verse in purple ink: *I have loved thee with an everlasting love.* Brenda held the card open for Christie to read, then set it on the windowsill, where it towered over all the others.

The other present was wrapped in a cardboard box, the shape of a wedge of Vermont cheese. Christie felt a tingle in her fingers. They wanted to tear that box open themselves, but her hand just lay there on the bed.

Brenda opened the box and took out something made of clear plastic. She got the birthday book from the chest and opened it to a story called "Christmas."

"Let's read to each other," she said. She slipped the open book between the clear plastic sheet and the slanted back and rested it on Christie's lap—a book holder! It was just right. Christie could read through the plastic. She'd need someone to turn pages, but the book wouldn't close up and fall on the bed or the floor.

"Thanks. I like." She smiled at Brenda. "Why you pick Chris story in June?"

"It's so hot outside, I want to read about something cold. The colder, the better."

"Doc Al says some stor too old for me. He says prob save til high school."

"Why did he bring it to you if it's too old?"

"For 'Rip Van Wink' and 'The Head Horse.' He read me and they good. You read, it sound bet."

The description of Christmas in England in earlier days had some words and things they had to guess about, but they understood most of it. "It like Scrooge and Tyn Tim," Christie told Brenda.

When she had finished reading, Brenda said, "I'll bring in two new paperbacks for you. You can use the stand and read those yourself. We can save this for a few more years. I think it's a little too grown-up for us."

Christie didn't mind. It didn't feel the same when Brenda read it out loud anyway. There had been something special in it when Dr. Alexander read to her, and she wanted to keep the book private.

She looked at the clock Grandpa had set on the chest. Brenda had time to do something Christie had been thinking about. She didn't want Grandma to know about it. "You write a let for me?" she asked.

"Sure. Where's the paper? Is there a pen in here?"

"In ches draw," Christie said. "Ask nurse pen."

Brenda ran out of the room and came back with a blue ball-point pen. She climbed up and sat on the edge of the bed, dangling her legs over the side. She pulled the tray stand over her knees, then wrote, "June 30th," at the top of a lined sheet of paper from Grandpa's notebook.

"Dear Benj," Christie began. Brenda wrote slowly, then looked up, waiting. Christie said the words she had been thinking about for so long, waiting after each two or three words for Brenda to write.

Although Christie said many words wrong, Brenda wrote them correctly. When they were done, she held the letter for Christie to read.

> Dear Benjamin,
> I miss you, too. I can't wait for you to come home. I can talk now, and one of these days, I'll get up and walk. When I do, I know Grandpa and Grandma will send for you, and Rusty will come to Sharpe to live with all of us.
> Remember what Daddy said? We are a family and we have to stick together. Don't forget.
> Have fun for me in California, okay?
> Brenda is writing this for me. She says Rusty is a good boy and even though his bed is on the floor in her bedroom, he sneaks up on her bed early every morning and lays his head on her belly.
> Lots of love and kisses from your sister,
> Christie.
> XXXXXXXXXXXXXXXXX000000000000000
> P.S. Write to me.

Brenda folded the paper into a rectangle. When she couldn't find an envelope, she said, "I'll take this home and use one of Mother's envelopes and a stamp. What about the address?"

Christie hadn't thought of that. "Look in draw for Benj let. May be on env."

Grandma, always neat and orderly, had kept Benjamin's letter in its envelope. In the upper left-hand corner, Brenda found a white label with the names Mr. and Mrs. William MacLane, followed by their Claremont address. She tore another sheet from the notebook and copied the address.

Christie laughed. "Put smile on my add. Smile face." The white label had a bright yellow face with a curved black-line smile, and Christie knew Benjamin would like one back.

Brenda had barely tucked the letter and the address into her pocket when the announcement telling visitors to leave came over the loudspeaker.

"See you next Sunday," Brenda said. "I rode my bike over today. I hope it's cooled off since noon."

When she had gone, Christie looked at the tall card on the windowsill. From here she could still see the purple ink of the Bible verse. They had talked about it in Sunday school, so the words were easy to remember. *I have loved thee with an everlasting love.* God wouldn't say that if He didn't mean it, she thought. And Grandpa seemed to be convinced of His love. But why—oh, it was hard to understand.

She shifted her gaze to the picture on her calendar. Grandpa had said that she could imagine herself jumping onto that bike and riding anywhere she wanted to go. He was right. Her trip always began on that shaded country road, and she rode out toward the sunshine. Today, her imagination took her to Claremont, California. She saw herself getting off the bike at a pink cottage, walking up to the door and lifting a gold knocker. When the door opened, there stood Benjamin, his suitcase in his hand and a grin on his face. "I knew you'd come!" he shouted. "I knew you'd come."

7

Jonathan's News

Were Dr. Alexander and Ellen lying to her? Her therapist kept exclaiming over the shape of her muscles. "See what happens when you help me?" she asked Christie one August morning. "I can just see those muscles getting stronger and stronger."

What good did it do? Did her toes move? Her hands? Why didn't they tell the truth? Even Grandpa and Grandma praised her for working so hard. Just because she was a kid, did they think she didn't know when they were giving her a snow job? Dad used to say those words when she or Benjamin stretched the truth.

She looked right at Ellen and said, "Ha! Ha! Ha! Joke!" Her slow-motion laugh came out just right, so Ellen knew it wasn't meant to be funny.

The therapist frowned. "I don't kid around about something this serious, young lady."

She seemed to mean it. Again, Christie felt some hope. She'd show them all!

That morning when Miss Whitaker pushed Jonathan's wheelchair in, Christie was concentrating so hard on her big toe that her eyes burned from staring at it.

The nurse didn't put the sneakers back on, and Christie was grateful. At least Jonathan wouldn't have to look at those tugboats.

He chuckled. "That la—ee lob till fight—ing you?"

Dr. Alexander had told him!

"Dr. Al—ec—an—der told me to do that too. I give that big toe the e—vil eye ev—ry day, but it tub—born. Let do it, o—kay?" Jonathan pulled his pajama leg up over his knee and looked down at his slippered foot. "I'm go—ing to move you, you la—ee lob," he said. When Christie didn't join in, he said it again. "I'm go—ing to move you, you la—ee lob."

Christie glared at her bare toe and said, "I'm go move you, you laz slob." She looked into Jonathan's brown eyes, and the silliness of their words struck them both at the same time. They laughed until tears came, until the line of words turned into a chant and got louder and louder. Their toes didn't move, but they were still yelling with laughter.

The door flew open and Miss Whitaker rushed into the room. "What's going on here?" she asked, looking worried.

They laughed some more. She looked so funny, standing there with her hands on her hips. Miss Whitaker relaxed, and then she couldn't help laughing too. Like the measles, their laughs were contagious. Christie hadn't laughed like this since before the accident.

By the time Grandpa and Grandma came in, they had settled down, and Grandma put Christie's sneakers back on. She didn't care. Not even those monsters could spoil the fun that had come into her room with Jonathan.

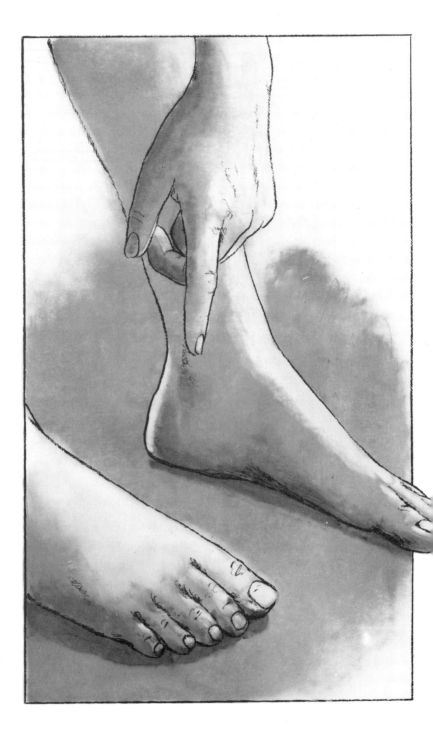

"I hear you two characters have been waking up this whole floor," Grandpa said. "Good for you!"

Grandma's eyes were sparkling.

Grandpa pushed Jonathan's wheelchair to the door and waited while Jonathan waved at Christie. "We'll give e—vil eye to—mor—row. O—kay?" Jonathan said.

Christie giggled again and Grandpa said, "I'd better get this clown out of here!"

One Sunday, Brenda pushed Christie's wheelchair to the porch where Jonathan was reading a mystery book. She brought along the calculator that Christie hadn't used yet. They started a game: Brenda made up number problems for Christie to figure out in her head, then Brenda checked the answer on the calculator.

Very fast, Brenda said, "How much are three plus two plus six plus three plus eight plus five, minus ten?"

Christie, who was good at math, kept up with her. Right away she knew the answer was seventeen. "Sev," she said.

"Uh-uh, the answer isn't seven. You're wrong."

Christie tried again, a little louder. "Sev."

"I said that's wrong." Brenda shook her head.

Jonathan was watching, looking right at Christie.

"Right?" Christie asked, expecting him to back her up. He knew what she meant.

He didn't speak.

Brenda had trapped her on purpose. Christie felt her face turn red. Brenda had made her look dumb in front of Jonathan.

"You don't try!" Brenda accused her.

Brenda doesn't understand, Christie thought. She treats me like a "special kid" now, like Oscar Snow. When I get back to school, I won't have to worry about being in the sixth grade. I'll be in the "special class." How can I ever stand it?

Jonathan closed his book. "Chri—tie. I have good new." He was trying to change the subject. She didn't ask him to tell her what he meant. He told her anyway.

"Nect week, I'm go—ing to a re—ha—bil—i—ta—ton ho—pi—tal down near Bo—ton. Dr. Al—ec—an—der think I'm rea—dy. They can help me more where I can have peech ther—a—py ev—ry day, and I'm go—ing to have op—er—a—ton on my feet. If my feet get bet—ter, they'll traight—en out thi thing." He lifted his bent wrist and stuck his tongue out at it.

Brenda laughed. Christie wanted to cry. She had never thought that Jonathan might leave the hospital before she did. Now he expected her to be glad for him.

She didn't look at him. "Take me back to my room, Bren, please," she said.

"Chri—tie. Be hap—py for me." Jonathan's voice followed her.

She turned her head away. They were supposed to be her friends, but friends were kind, weren't they? These two didn't care how she felt. Jonathan was leaving and he was glad. No wonder. They were going to fix him up, but Christie was staying here playing a silly game that couldn't fix anything! She closed her eyes tight. Tears were prickling behind her eyelids, and the deep pain had hit the pit of her stomach again.

Brenda pushed the wheelchair toward the hall. Jonathan called, "I'll be down to—mor—row."

"Let's watch TV." Brenda stopped at the door of the television room, where a few patients and visitors sat.

"No. Room, please."

Brenda left the wheelchair near the bed and went to find Miss Whitaker. As soon as the nurse had lifted Christie back into bed, she said, "Tired," and closed her eyes again. Brenda must have waited. But after a while, Christie heard the door open and whir closed.

When she knew she was alone, she talked to God. "You said You loved me. But You're taking Jonathan away." She'd almost forgotten about the verse on her card, but now its words drifted into her mind. *I have loved thee with an everlasting love.* Still, the tears ran down her face, across her ear lobes, and dripped onto the pillow.

She didn't eat any supper, just held her lips together when Mrs. Williams, the evening nurse, tried to feed her. If she could have, she would have pushed the tray away, and she felt an odd tingling in her hand when she thought about it.

After Mrs. Williams had gone, Phil, a male nurse, rolled Jonathan's wheelchair close to Christie's bed. When he left, Jonathan said, "We got to talk, Chri—tie."

She knew her eyes were red. Her supper was on the tray.

"I'll write, Chri—tie, on my type—writ—er. You can dic—tate let—ter to me and have Bren—da write."

Jonathan reached his bent hand toward her and Christie felt that tingling in her right hand again. She felt her eyes pop wide open when the hand moved. She watched it move across the sheet to touch Jonathan's hand. She could feel his warmth.

They stared at each other. She was crying again. So was he. Then they both laughed.

"You mon—key. You moved your hand. I jut knew it! You can do an—y—thing."

Jonathan rang the buzzer, and the evening nurse came in. While Mrs. Williams watched, Christie moved her hand back to her side, then out to the edge of the mattress.

The nurse hugged her and went to the door. "Page Dr. Alexander. I saw him on the porch a while ago. Christie moved her hand!"

Once more, the room filled up with people who had to be shooed away by a grinning Dr. Alexander. They seemed ready to stay all night, watching Christie move her hand and her arm.

When Jonathan, Christie, and Dr. Alexander were the only ones left in the room, the doctor picked up the telephone and asked the operator for Grandpa's number in Sharpe. Someone answered and the doctor said, "You tell him, Miss Van Winkle." He held the phone to her ear and mouth.

"Tell me what?" Grandpa wanted to know.

"I move hand, Gram," she yelled in his ear.

"Yahoo!" he hollered back.

Grandma must have taken the telephone away from him. "Who *is* this?" she said.

"Chris. I move hand, Gram!" Without a warning, her head turned to the right in the collar and she looked at Jonathan. "My head, Gram! My head!"

"Put Dr. Alexander on, Christie. I thought you said 'hand'; now you say, 'head.' "

"You talk, Doc Al," Christie said.

He took the phone and talked to both grandparents. By now, Grandpa was on the bedroom extension and Christie could hear his shout right through the telephone. "Praise the Lord!"

She was sliding her hand back and forth, back and forth on the sheet, following it with her eyes and her head at the same time. Like Grandma, she was so happy she cried.

By the time Mrs. Williams came back, Christie had eaten everything on her tray, even the melted ice cream. Jonathan had left with the words, "I'll bring you a new friend to—mor—row. You'll like him."

It was hard to go to sleep. Christie kept moving her hand and rolling her head from left to right, then right to left. It felt good. Her neck grated and made a creaking sound in her head. That must have happened to Rip Van Winkle, too.

The next morning Jonathan came to visit. Pushing his wheelchair was a short, plump man. "Thi Mark Wig—gin, Chri—tie. Peech ther—a—pit. Dr. Al—ec—an—der want him work with you. He'll help you make good peech. He help me talk fat—ter."

Mark's round face was tanned, and he had smiling gray eyes. His hair was just about the same light brown as hers, and short too. Even though he was kind of fat, he moved easily. She liked him already.

After he left, she took stock. She had two therapists, her grandparents, Brenda, Dr. Alexander, Miss Whitaker, Mrs. Williams, a head and hand and arm that could move by themselves, plus mystery rides with her DARTMOUTH sweat shirt on. And . . . her eyes strayed to the purple card on the windowsill.

Perhaps she could be glad for Jonathan, after all.

8

<u>Bye, Pal</u>

It wasn't long after Christie first moved her hand that the other hand moved, and, although she didn't mention it to Jonathan, she was thankful that neither of her hands was bent at the wrist.

She had wanted to try everything at once, even though Grandma warned, "One step at a time, Christie. You mustn't overdo it."

"Fiddle!" Grandpa said. "Who knows what God may be doing? Let her try anything she can, Elizabeth."

Holding a pencil wasn't easy, but she could press the keys of the calculator. Her grasp was weak and her writing big and shaky, like Benjamin's had been in the first grade, or like her own used to be when she tried to write with her left hand. Wouldn't Benjamin laugh when he saw her scribbling?

She had been disappointed when his second letter came, because Aunt Harriet must have checked his words. Nothing was spelled wrong, and he didn't mention coming home. In fact, he hadn't told her much at all. If he'd had to copy it over to make that nice, neat page, it couldn't have been much fun, either.

Grandpa had carried Christie over to the calendar and placed the red pen in her hand so she could draw a circle around September ninth, the day her hand and her head had first moved.

One day Dr. Alexander put the DARTMOUTH sweat shirt over her pajama top, set her in the wheelchair, and pushed her directly to the elevator. Waiting inside, with Phil behind his wheelchair, was Jonathan.

Christie knew he was leaving today for the rehabilitation center in Massachusetts, but she thought she'd already said her good-bye in her room that morning.

"I have to wave to my pal," Jonathan said. He was grinning, but there was sadness in his brown eyes.

When the elevator reached the first floor, the two chairs were wheeled through the waiting area to the front doors where Miss Whitaker and Jonathan's parents waited. Dr. Alexander pushed her outside into the chilly fall air and left her chair on the top step while he and Phil lifted Jonathan onto the back seat of his family car.

"Bye, pal." He waved from the open window.

"Bye, Jon; I write."

While they waved, the car rounded the traffic circle and disappeared over the rim of the hill. Jonathan was gone. The pain was back in the pit of her stomach. In her lap, her hand covered a small package Jonathan had put there while they were in the elevator.

Dr. Alexander pulled the wheelchair backwards up the two steps into the waiting area, turned right, and entered a door under a sign that said COFFEE SHOP. People were sitting on stools at the counter or in chairs at round tables. The doctor pushed Christie's wheelchair close to a table from which she could see the whole shop and the door. She could even look down into the hospital gift shop, one step below the dining area.

"Pick anything you want from that list, Christie. There's another list of specials over there on the wall."

By the time the volunteer in the pink smock came to their table, Christie was ready.

"Or ice cream, choc surp, marsh and nuts. Cher on top, please." Her mouth watered.

"Oreo," Dr. Alexander explained, when the volunteer looked at him. He ordered a vanilla milk shake, and the lady went behind the counter to build Christie's sundae.

"We'll celebrate for Jonathan. He's taking the next step that will help him to get back to college." Dr. Alexander tucked a paper napkin into the neck band of her sweat shirt.

Since she had started using her hands, getting food to her mouth was a struggle. She kept spilling things onto her pajamas and the bedding until the nurses thought of pushing the tray stand close to her stomach. Now, most of the spills went back into her dish.

Grandpa and Grandma were there when they got back to Christie's room. Grandma clucked her tongue. "Look at you! I'll have to wash that sweat shirt."

The dribbles of marshmallow and chocolate syrup were drying on the dark green shirt. "Don't worry about it," the doctor said. "My old sweat shirt has been washed five hundred times. They're tough."

"Looks like my girl has been pigging out." Grandpa chuckled.

Grandma smiled, but she said, "If she can't eat her dinner, you've only yourself to blame." She scolded the doctor just as she would have Christie or Benjamin.

That evening while Christie waited for Mrs. Williams to come and turn off the light, she untied the ribbon on the package and tore off the yellow paper. Inside the small white box, she found a slender gold chain, coiled on a wad of cotton. Centered on the chain, tiny gold letters spelled out I CAN DO ANYTHING.

Mrs. Williams fastened the necklace at the back of Christie's neck, and then, when the light was out and the door closed, Christie put the palm of one hand flat across the letters. A feeling like homesickness started the pain in her stomach,

and she tried to imagine the days without Jonathan. "God," she said, "why are You taking away the people I love? First Mom and Dad, and Benjamin, and now Jonathan."

Even though she knew Benjamin and Jonathan were very much alive, they were far away and she couldn't see them. Rusty was right in this same town but she couldn't see him, either. She thought of Dr. Alexander, then pushed the future away. It would be a long, long time before she lost him too.

Mark, the speech therapist, came every week on Monday, Wednesday, and Friday. So far, the activities were more like games than work, and she couldn't see that her speech had improved, either. She remembered that Jonathan had still not been able to say his "s" sounds when he left, and she wondered whether Mark could really help her talk like she could before the accident.

He had begun by testing her to find out what her problems were. "So we won't waste time on the good guys," he told her. From the bright red manual with a white title *For Speech Sake!*, he read a list of words. She tried to repeat them after him. With one-syllable words, she was good, but when the words had more than one, she said the first syllable and stopped, every time. She let out a sigh of impatience.

"Red wagon," Mark read.

"Red wag."

"Yellow flower."

"Yel flow."

"Cherry pie."

"Cher pie." This was silly. Why was he making her look so dumb?

As if he read her thoughts, Mark said, "I know you think this is foolish. Sure, I could tell when you said, 'red wagon,' that you were having trouble with more than one syllable, but be patient—I'm listening for other things, too, like sounds."

"Little lamb."

"Lit lamb."

"My chair."

"My chai."

"New bicycle."

"New bice."

"Seven sisters."

"Sev sis."

"Sugar."

"Sug."

"Sun."

"Sun." The list went on and on, and Mark did not correct her. He made notes on a chart he had prepared before he came to her room.

Finally, Mark closed the book and slipped the chart inside the front cover. "You're in good shape, Christie. You said all the sounds perfectly—did you know? That will make our job easier."

"But I talk dumb."

"If you were dumb, Christie, you couldn't talk. That's what dumb really means, you know, not being able to talk at all."

"Well, then, I talk stupe."

Mark's voice sharpened. "Let's understand each other right now. You don't fuss and complain or put yourself down. That will interfere with our progress. When I go down to see Jonathan next week, I want to tell him how much you've improved, not how much you've grouched."

Mark was scolding her, and she didn't even know him very well. She blinked to keep from crying. It seemed that she'd done a lot of crying in this place.

"What do you like to do, Christie?"

Now he wanted her to forget that he was mean. Did he think she was a little kid?

He waited.

"I like bice." Christie looked up at her poster-calendar on the wall.

Mark went closer to it. "What a wonderful place to be. Can't you just imagine the sounds you'd hear if you stopped your bicycle and sat there in the shade at the side of the road? Let's see, I'd hear birds, all kinds of birds."

Christie was interested. "Crows?"

Mark made a face. "They're loud and sassy. *Caw! Caw!*" His imitation—noisy, raspy and sudden—made Christie's head turn.

She laughed. "A squir. *Ch, ch, ch, ch, ch, ch.*"

"Frogs. *Ri—vet, ri—vet.*" Christie couldn't believe it; Mark sounded just like a bullfrog.

"Crick." Her "*ee, ee, ee, eee*" brought Mark to his feet. "That did it! I'm getting out of this forest. Next thing I know, I'll hear a bear."

Her second speech lesson turned out to be a music class. They sang.

Mark said, "You say, 'Old MacDonald,' Christie."

Her eyes must have told him she was going to get him. "Old Mac, Chris."

"Joker!" Mark shook an index finger at her. "Come on, smarty, say, 'Old MacDonald.' "

"Old Mac."

"This time, you do what I do." He sang, "Old Mac-Don-ald" and stopped. She expected him to go on and finish "had a farm." But he didn't.

"You sing, Christie. 'Old Mac-Don-ald.' "

"I fee goof."

"Never mind, sing."

"Old Mac-Don-ald." She barely sang the words loudly enough for him to hear.

"Wonderful! Do it again."

"Old Mac-Don-ald." This time it was a little louder.

"Let's try the whole thing. Listen. 'Old Mac-Don-ald had a chick-en, ee-igh, ee-igh, oh.' " He waited for her to sing.

He had put an extra syllable on 'chick.' He was trying to catch her. She sang, "Old Mac-Don-ald had a chick-en, ee-igh, ee-igh, oh."

"Super! You sang *Donald* and *chicken,* two syllables each. Did you know that?"

"Let's do more."

Mark thought, then he sang, "Old Mac-Don-ald had a kit-ten, ee-igh, ee-igh, oh."

It was easy—she could put syllables together!

Then Mark spoiled everything. "You say it this time, Christie. 'Old MacDonald had a chicken, ee-igh, ee-igh, oh.' "

She spoke the words, "Old Mac had a chick, ee-igh, ee-igh, oh." If she could sing them, why couldn't she say them? She pounded her fist on the mattress.

Mark ignored that. "Just what I expected. Don't worry, if you can sing it, you can say it, someday. You'll see."

"We'll try something new this time while we sing. Watch me." Mark sang, "Old Mac-Don-ald had a kit-ten, ee-igh, ee-igh, oh." At the same time, he clapped his hands in rhythm with each syllable, making the second syllable of *kitten* louder than the other.

"Come on, Christie. Clap so hard on the second syllable of *kitten* that it hurts."

They sang and clapped, thumping out that last syllable. It was fun, and Christie was pleased with herself.

Then Mark spoiled it again. "Talk the words this time and clap the same way."

She tried to do what he said, but it was like trying to pat her head and rub her stomach; it just didn't work. Every time she made the loud clap, there was no syllable sound. She always closed her mouth after *kit.*

She was glad when he looked at his watch and said, "Time to go. Will you practice saying and clapping those words when you can? I'll be back Friday. Don't be discouraged, okay?"

Another line? Like her big toe? After he left she pounded at the mattress, imagining that it was Mark's nose, and it made her feel less angry.

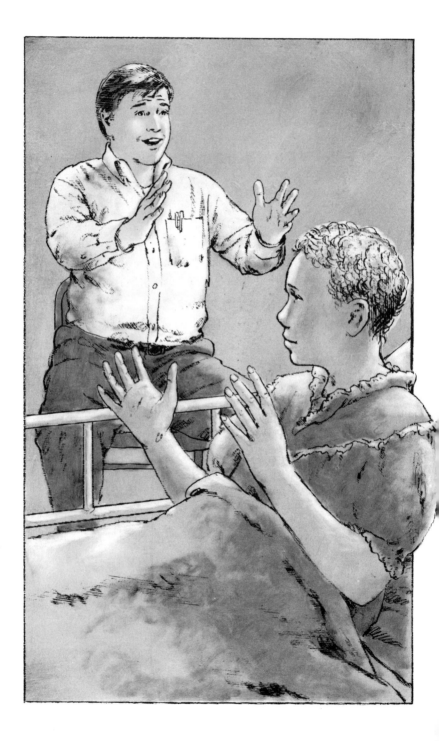

How many times had she talked to her toe, that lazy slob, with no success? How come her hands and her head moved, but her feet and legs didn't, no matter how much she concentrated on them? She hadn't even spoken to her hands and neck, and they had moved on their own. Maybe she should give up that silly game, and her feet might move by themselves. Now Mark had her playing another game.

True to his word, Jonathan sent her a letter every week. He said the therapy was hard and he was working out in a special room with machines that helped him to move. He told her about a whirlpool bath; it sounded like fun. He liked his therapists and nurses, and he had two doctors. One was a surgeon who did operations. Jonathan ended his letters with a big circle on which he drew eyes, a nose, and a wide, smiling mouth. Under that he typed, "You can do anything."

When he told her that, she believed it. Believing was a lot different from *doing*.

Ever since Mrs. Williams had fastened the gold necklace around her neck, Christie hadn't let anyone take it off, not even when she had a bath.

9

Not Ready

"You like your bicycle, Christie. What else do you like?"

"I like woods. Someday I'll be fors."

Mark didn't ask questions. He thought a long time, then he smiled. "A forester. You want to be a forester."

"That's right, a fors."

"Remember how you used to sing your ABCs? I'll bet you had trouble saying them without slipping into the song."

She couldn't remember doing that herself, but she could remember Benjamin singing the alphabet every time he practiced at home.

"Sing after me, 'a-b-c-d-e-f-g.' "

Christie giggled. She felt like a first-grade kid, but she sang, "a-b-c-d-e-f-g."

"Good. Keep that tune in your head and be my echo again. 'I will be a for-es-ter.' "

"I will be a for-es-ter." Christie sang without a mistake.

"Right on the nozzle." Mark looked pleased. "Sing it again."

"I will be a for-es-ter." It was easy.

"Remember that tune in your mind, but *say* the words. Keep that rhythm."

"I will be a for-es-ter."

"Okay!" Mark made a circle of his thumb and index finger, and held the other three fingers in the air, a sign of approval.

Christie liked that. She brought her thumb and finger together and said, "O-kay."

"You did it. It was a song."

"Jo-ker," she teased him. The word had a musical rhythm, and Christie wondered if she'd always think of tunes when she spoke words of more than one syllable.

"Practice, practice, practice," Mark said, "and before you realize it, your words will go together like pines and needles."

"You mean pins and nee-dles."

"No, Miss Forester, I definitely mean pines and needles."

She got it! Pine needles!

"Some poems have rhythm, just like music. How would you like to learn one about your forest?" He had his red speech book open to a page near the back. "First, listen and enjoy the whole thing while I read it to you."

The Heart of the Wild

The heart of the wild is an interesting place.
There are so many things to see.
The golden eagle in the tallest tree,
And the flight of the bumblebee.

The heart of the wild has secret pools
Where the velvety cattails grow.
And the bright mallard ducks rise up from the
*   swamp.*
They take to the wing just so.

If you've never wandered out there in the wild,
You've missed a most interesting time.
For nature is better to watch than a show,
And you'll leave your troubles behind.

While she listened, Christie had been in the forest. She decided that she liked the poem so much, someday she'd put it in her journal. "Can I have a co-py?"

"I'll bring one the next time I come, and we'll learn it by heart," Mark promised.

They practiced the poem for a while, but Christie concentrated so hard on *in-ter-est-ing, man-y, gold-en, ea-gle, tall-est,* and *bum-ble-bee,* she only had time to learn the first verse.

"Where's your red pen?" Mark asked.

Christie pointed to the chest, and Mark took the pen to the calendar and circled the date. "That's for your new words. See you in two days, Christie."

When he had gone, Christie sang to the alphabet tune: "I'm go-ing to move you, you la-zy slob." Her toe didn't move, but she was getting used to that.

When Grandpa came, he carried in a leather case. It was heavy—Christie could tell by the effort he used to lift it up to the chest. He pushed on the fasteners and the cover popped open. A pale blue typewriter!

Grandma cleared the tray stand, then Grandpa placed the typewriter on the tray and plugged it in. He pushed the stand close to her.

"There, sweetie. Now you can write your own letters to Benjamin and Jonathan. Letters should be private."

He set out white typing paper and correcting tape and rolled a sheet of paper into the roller. As he turned around, he saw the red circle on the calendar. "A red-letter day? What did we miss this time?"

She hadn't thought of it before, but it did seem that her big moments always happened when someone other than her grandparents was with her.

Christie heard the ABC tune in her head, and she said, "Thank you, Grand-pa, ver-y much." It sounded like poetry when she said it.

Grandpa smacked kisses on her cheek, and Grandma pecked the other one. "You'll soon be our old Christie," she declared, and she clucked her tongue with pleasure. She bustled about, putting away pajamas she had washed and tidying drawers that didn't need it.

Right now, Christie didn't want to write letters—that was something she'd do when she was alone. For now, she was happy to type whatever came to her mind. She typed what she could remember of the poem.

The Heart of the Wild

The heart of the wild is an interesting place,
there are so many things to see,
the golden eegel in the tallest tree
and the flite of the bumblebee.

Like a piano player, she wiggled her tired index fingers when she had finished. One good thing about being so slow was that she had time to think, so she didn't make many mistakes.

"I'll bet we can find a table that will fit in front of your wheelchair. That would be more comfortable than a jiggly tray stand." Grandpa wasn't one to waste time when he had an idea. He turned and left the room.

Grandma was knitting in her rocking chair. The half-finished brown mitten with yellow stripes must be for her, Christie thought. Benjamin and her cousins wouldn't need those out in California.

"Want to read a po-em?" Christie asked.

Grandma got up, leaned over, and read the paragraph. "That's nice. Maybe we should bring you a dictionary."

Christie nodded.

Grandpa was back, pushing a wheelchair. He lifted her into it, covered her knees with the blanket from the closet, then disappeared out the door again, leaving her sitting there.

"Now, what's that man up to?" Grandma asked.

Christie knew, but her grandmother didn't listen when she was knitting and counting stitches, so she probably hadn't heard Grandpa mention the table.

This time, when he returned he pushed the door back as far as it would go so a maintenance man could carry in a long metal table. The man looked at Christie. "Is this the lady who ordered the table?"

"She's the one," Grandpa told him. "Just set it right in front of her, and thanks a jillion." He always had a different number of thanks, sometimes a zillion, sometimes a billion and sometimes a trillion. No boring millions for him.

After Grandpa set the typewriter on the table, Christie tried it. It was too high.

"No problem," the maintenance man assured them. He knelt down, took a wrench from his back pocket and loosened some screws on the legs. The table slid down until it was the right height; then he retightened the screws. "Adjustable, just like that," he explained. "You going to write a book?"

Christie smiled. "May-be." She could almost hear Jonathan telling her, "You can do anything."

As soon as the man left, Christie said, "Like to read Mark's po-em?"

Grandpa read the words on her paper. "I like that; I hope there's more. Did Mark write it?"

"It's in our speech book." She added, "Mark will teach me more. He's co-py-ing it."

"Good, we'll say it together, like singing in the car." Grandpa looked as if he felt good; his eyes were bright today. The deep sadness would be back, Christie expected, but for now, he was happy.

It was the same with her. She could be happy one minute, then the pain would be back in her stomach the next. She had thought about that and tried to figure it out. Different things brought the pain back; she never knew what they would be. Words could do it, like Grandpa's "Fiddle!" Mom said that too, when she didn't believe something. Food, like Dad's favorite, roast beef and gravy, or Benjamin's, hamburgers, could bring tears. Even a smell, like the day Grandma had brought a bouquet of purple lilacs into the room. She remembered how Mom loved the smell of lilacs and carried one around while she worked so she could sniff it once in a while.

It must be the same for Grandpa and Grandma. Grandma didn't sniff and cry now, like she had when Christie first woke up, but sometimes she stopped knitting or sewing and just stared down at her hands.

The happy times were like a great relief from pain. Funny though, even during those times, she had started to feel guilty. She had no right to be laughing and enjoying herself when Mom and Dad were dead. She wished she could talk to Grandpa about that, but she didn't want to make him more unhappy. Maybe later on.

She saw her grandfather looking at her. Near the bottom of the paper, she typed, "I love you, Grandpa."

She signaled with her finger and he came over to look. "Me too, sweetie, me too," he told her. He did some signaling with his eyebrows and his head, in Grandma's direction.

Christie understood. Slowly she typed, "I love you, Grandma."

"Come see this, Elizabeth," Grandpa said.

"Just one minute, I don't want to drop this stitch. Eleven, twelve," she counted. She sighed, got up, and walked over to look down at the words. At first, she didn't notice the last words, but when she did, she smiled. She twisted the roller knob once and typed, "I love you, Christie." After she turned away, Grandpa chuckled and finished the line with "XXXXXXXXXXXXXXXXXXXXXXX."

Back in bed, Christie looked at her grandparents. Grandpa was reading the paper while he sat in a straight chair near the window, and Grandma was knitting on the mitten again, her mouth moving every so often as she counted. She made

Christie lots of clothes, and she also did that for Benjamin and her cousins. She and the ladies of her church did knitting for poor children too.

When her grandparents had gone down to the coffee shop, Dr. Alexander came in. "Know what day next Wednesday is?" he asked. He didn't wait for her to answer. He began to sing, "Over the river and through the woods, to Grand-mother's house we go."

Christie just looked at him, waiting. What did he want her to say?

He touched the new typewriter. "A handsome thing, Miss Van Winkle. You'll use it a lot after you get home next week."

She was going home next week? Her heart pounded and she had to breathe fast. The pounding was in her head and her ears now, beating hard, like a pulse.

"But, I'm not read-y! I can't walk yet!"

The doctor sat on the edge of her bed. "I know. We've talked it over and decided that you might progress even faster at home. And now it's time for me to tell you the first most important thing."

He paused, then he asked, "Do you know what a miracle is?"

Christie thought about that. "It's when some-thing hap-pens that ev-er-y-one thought was im-pos-si-ble."

Dr. Alexander nodded. "A miracle has already happened because of your spirit. You are talking again, and you can move your hands and arms."

"Yes, and be-fore you know it, my toe will move, then my legs, and I'll be out of that chair." She shot him a questioning glance.

"Because you are so strong, Christie, I can tell you this. We have not been able to find out why your legs don't move. It's possible they may never move. That's why you must do every good thing you can with your life—right from that chair."

Christie's eyes burned, and she felt her stomach quiver. She drew in a shaky breath as Dr. Alexander reached for her hand. "Mom and Dad are dead, and I can't walk," she said. "Why did God do this to me? Why does-n't He lis-ten when I ask Him to make me well?"

"He listens, Christie. If you want an answer, you must change your question. Don't ask, 'Why?' Ask, 'What can I do about it?' "

Christie thought about that. She didn't wonder so much anymore whether God loved her. But she had hoped that He would fix her legs.

Dr. Alexander squeezed her hand. "The first most important thing is to remember that miracles still happen. Never let go of that thought. Remember the miracles God has already done. And knowing you, I'm certain that no one can keep you from fighting to walk again."

He smiled at her and stood up. Through shimmering tears, she watched Grandpa and Grandma come back into the room. She saw Dr. Alexander nod at them and leave.

She felt the pain in her stomach and the pounding in her ears and head. She swallowed, and it made a loud, gulping sound. As if she were a little kid, Grandpa lifted her from the bed and carried her to Grandma's rocking chair. He sat down, and she felt Grandma tuck the blanket around her legs.

While Grandpa rocked and held her close, she cried. She cried for a house without Mom and Dad and Benjamin and

Rusty. She cried about leaving the safety of this room, this third floor. She cried about leaving her friends, Brenda, Miss Whitaker, Mrs. Williams, Ellen, Mark, and most of all, Dr. Alexander. She cried about sitting in a wheelchair or lying in bed while other kids went to school or played. She cried about missing Jonathan, about being left behind her classmates. She cried about sleeping in Mom's old room and about butting into Grandpa's and Grandma's lives.

Too tired to cry anymore, she quieted while Grandpa smoothed her hair and dried her face with his clean handkerchief.

It had been months since she'd closed her eyes to get away from hurt and pain. She did it now.

10

Good-bye, Brenda

The next day it seemed that some of her sorrow had been washed away by her tears. Her problems were still there, her losses were great for a twelve-year-old to bear, but she had started to think ahead to her new life.

Lately, Grandpa and Grandma had not come to the hospital every single day. She realized now that they had been doing things at home in Sharpe, preparing for her arrival. She wanted to ask about Rusty—could he come too? But she knew a dog would make more work for two old people. Maybe after Benjamin came back. . . .

On Saturday, Dr. Alexander made one of his special visits, bringing a powered wheelchair that she could operate herself. By moving what Dr. Alexander called the 'joystick', she could turn the chair to the left, the right, or around in a circle. She could work the brake. Maybe, someday, when her arms and shoulders were stronger, she could get herself into the chair from her bed, then back to the bed again.

"You can take this chair home with you if you promise to obey the traffic laws. No wheelies and no racing," the doctor warned with a grin.

He took her sweat shirt from a drawer while they talked, then handed it to her. "You'll be coming back to see me every month, and I want you to wear this so I can keep track of how fast you grow and get you a bigger one someday."

She would still be seeing her "Doc Al!" Although she could singsong his last name, she would always call him by her own special nickname.

It took time, but she managed to pull the sweat shirt over her head and down around her hips. Finally she was ready.

"You drive," he said. Her steering was wobbly, and the chair moved along the corridor in a zigzag course.

"To the elevators," he directed. "Can you reach the 'up' button?"

Because it was down low, she could, and they waited for a car to rise from the ground floor, the lighted numbers showing its progress. After she rolled inside, he said, "Over here. Press number four."

She had been on the first floor to see Jonathan off, she had explored the coffee shop and gift shop, and she had visited the nursery, but they had never taken a mystery trip to the fourth floor.

The corridor was identical to the one below, but she didn't recognize any of the nurses and attendants. "Turn left," the doctor told her.

A set of double doors swept open at their approach. Inside, children turned to look at her. Some lay in beds along both sides of the long room, and others sat in chairs or sprawled on a blue rug at the far end. There were shelves of books, toys, and games under the windowsills.

A glassed-in cubicle held a crib with an excited little boy who reached his arms out to Dr. Alexander. The doctor poked his head into the room and said, "Hi, Danny, you scoundrel. Give me a kiss." The child hugged his neck and pushed his nose into the doctor's cheek.

"Hi, Dr. Alexander, come see me, come see me," other children shouted at him.

"Meet Christie, my friend just like you guys," he said.

She knew that the funny feeling she got meant she was jealous. Doc Al was her special doctor, and she had never thought about him paying attention to any other kids. She knew he saw adult patients, but that hadn't bothered her. It hadn't even mattered that he was Jonathan's doctor.

They moved down the middle of the room, between the rows of beds. "You can stay for a while, Miss Van Winkle. Think you can find your way back to the elevator and down to the third floor by yourself?"

She knew she could. As the doctor disappeared through the swinging doors, a boy called to her. "Come over here, kid." He was about her age, with black hair and dark brown eyes. She steered her wheelchair to his bedside. "What's the matter with your legs?" he asked.

"I had an ac-ci-dent and I can't walk, not yet." She was curious too. "Why are you here?"

"I had my appendix out." He moved back carefully to lean against his pillow on the elevated head of the bed. "Want to play a game?"

She had thought of talking to those younger girls on the blue rug, but the boy's eyes made her think of Benjamin's when he teased her to play with him. "O-kay."

"You talk funny." Probably he didn't mean to hurt her feelings. "Accident too?"

"Right. What you want to play?"

"Chinese Checkers. You can get them over there on a shelf. Hey, Short Stuff, give Christie the Chinese Checkers."

She steered her chair to the blue rug and a small girl handed her the box. Christie saw that she wore a bandage taped over her left eye. The other eye was very gray, very bright.

"Did you hurt your eye?"

"My eye is gone," the girl told her. Christie sucked in a deep breath. The little girl wasn't fussing or crying; she seemed used to the idea, but Christie was shocked.

"What's your name?"

"Hester Thornton."

"I'm Chris-tie Ev-ans. Are you Short Stuff?"

"Bill likes to call me that. I don't care."

"Come on, Christie." Bill was in a hurry to get started.

"Want to watch us play?" invited Christie.

Hester trotted after the wheelchair, climbed up over the lowered side rails on Bill's bed, and leaned against the metal footboard. She adjusted her bathrobe over her knees.

"Don't wiggle, Short Stuff," Bill ordered.

They played one game and Bill won. Christie felt tired from the strain of lifting her arms and fingers up to the mattress top to move the marbles. She was relieved when a nurse came in and said, "I'm supposed to tell Christie Evans to go back down to her room. It's four-thirty, time to get ready for supper."

Kids called, "Good-bye, Christie. Come back."

In her room, she pressed the buzzer attached to the sheet, thinking how good it felt to be able to do that without any help. Mrs. Williams put her back in bed, then rolled her wheelchair into the corner. Christie would surprise Brenda tomorrow when she drove herself to the porch and the TV room.

Her Sundays always felt like holidays. No therapy, no cleaning lady, no Grandpa and Grandma. Brenda's afternoon visits made the day special.

This morning she had typed a letter to Benjamin to tell him about going home. She wanted Brenda to mail it so Grandma wouldn't see what she wrote. Her last paragraph was like a promise.

> It won't be long now. Once I get there, I should walk soon and they'll be sending for you right away. I can't wait to see you. Maybe we'll all drive over to Brenda's to get Rusty, after you get here.

She had just folded the paper and found an envelope in the chest when Dr. Alexander came in. "Hello, Miss Van Winkle, you look alluring today." Like Grandpa, he used unusual words that could make her laugh. Yesterday, she had been enticing, and she could remember being charming and having a magnetic personality. She tried to outdo him.

"And you are quite temp-ting your-self." He chuckled after that one.

"How was your visit to Pediatrics?"

"What's Pe-di-a-trics?" she asked.

"It's a branch of medicine dealing with children."

"Why didn't they put me in Pe-di-a-trics in-stead of this room?" She had wondered about that.

"It was better for you to be here, where your grandparents could stay all day. After you got out of Intensive Care, you needed the quiet. And the children in Pediatrics come and go all the time. We knew it would be hard for you to see them going home, over and over again."

She understood. Actually, she liked her safe, pink room. "What's In-ten-sive Care?"

"It's a special room where nurses are with you every minute when you are very sick. You don't remember that, because you were asleep all the time you were there, in the coma." Long ago, Grandpa had explained that word.

Dr. Alexander jumped up. "I'd better move along to Mr. Ketcham's room, or he'll be roaring like a tornado. Have a good afternoon with Brenda. I wish you could take her up to visit Pediatrics, but that would be squeezing the rules too far, I'm afraid."

Sometimes she believed he had ESP. How did he know she had planned to take Brenda to the fourth floor?

Brenda's last visit was a mixture of sadness and fun. She loved the wheelchair. "Can I try it after you get back in bed?"

"Why not? We'll make sure Mrs. Williams is busy with her pills first."

They went to the porch and watched visitors arrive, they saw part of a bowling tournament on TV, and Christie sat at the typewriter with Brenda beside her in another chair. While

Christie fiddled with the poem Mark had copied, Brenda played with the calculator. They changed places, Christie rolling the wheelchair away from the typewriter so Brenda could make a copy of the poem for herself.

Soon after three o'clock Miss Whitaker came in, her coat over her arm. She was going off duty. She carried two plastic containers with snap-on covers. "A treat from the coffee shop," she said, laying two wrapped straws on the table. "I'll miss you, Brenda. See you tomorrow, Christie." Together they sipped the strawberry milk shakes, enjoying them right down to the last noisy slurps. They counted the pieces of strawberries they sucked up through the straws, and Christie had two less than Brenda.

"Wrapper race?" Brenda challenged.

They wiped their straws and worked the wrappers back on to within an inch of the ends.

Brenda counted, "One, two, three, blow." They blew mightily through the straws, and the wrappers sailed across the room, toward the windows. Christie's went to the wall and dropped to the floor, and Brenda's stopped under the rocking chair where Grandma always sat. Finally Brenda threw the containers, straws, and wrappers into the wastebasket. "What'll we do now?"

"I want to walk."

Brenda looked uncomfortable. "I know."

"I mean it. I want you to help me walk." Christie had thought about trying to stand, but no one had suggested she do that yet.

"They'll have my ears if I get you out of that chair!" But Brenda was interested, Christie could tell.

"Come on. You scared?"

Christie backed her chair away from the table and drove it to the space in front of her bed. She locked the brake, then held her arms out to Brenda. "Lift me up."

She knew that Brenda had watched the nurses and her grandparents when they lifted her from the bed or a chair. This might be harder since she was almost as big as Brenda. Brenda stared at her, then bent forward and pulled Christie's hands until the top of her body was leaning ahead in the chair. Very fast, she pushed her hands under Christie's armpits and lifted and pulled at the same time. It was awkward and took all her strength. Brenda moaned when she bumped her shin on the metal footrest.

Christie knew she must be as heavy as a sack of cement, and just about as helpful. Brenda heaved and grunted until she had dragged Christie away from the chair. But then she kept moving backward, unable to stop, losing her balance. Christie felt them both falling, slow motion, until Brenda landed flat on her back on the hard tiles with Christie on top of her.

Brenda's eyes were closed, but Christie thought her own must be popping out like a frog's. Then Brenda's eyes opened, right below Christie's, and they both burst into giggles, louder and louder, until they were hiccupping and gasping. Brenda worked Christie off her body and onto her back on the floor.

Before they could decide what to do next, Mrs. Williams rushed into the room. When she saw Christie on the floor, she turned white. "Oh, no, Christie! Are you hurt?"

Christie didn't feel like laughing anymore. She felt foolish, in fact, lying there on her back, helpless. The hard tiles hurt her spine, and she knew she had done a dumb thing.

By now, Brenda was standing up, and she looked scared.

The nurse lifted Christie up and put her on the bed. "What in heaven's name were you doing?"

"It's my fault," Brenda said.

"It's my fault," echoed Christie.

"You might have broken a leg, or an arm, or cracked your head." Mrs. Williams was sputtering, like Grandma did when she was terribly worried. "You could have undone all the progress of the last year. How do you think your grandparents would feel if they came in and found you on the floor?"

Neither girl dared to speak.

The nurse turned to Brenda. "Are you all right?" Quickly Brenda explained what had happened, and the nurse seemed to calm down. "You must have landed pretty hard," she said to Brenda.

Brenda might have some black and blue marks, but Christie thought her friend was probably more embarrassed than hurt.

"Dr. Alexander has gone for the day, but I'll get Dr. Heath to come in and take a look at you," Mrs. Williams said. "You girls say your good-byes, and Christie can rest before supper—in bed, where I know she's safe."

After she left, the girls relaxed.

Christie hated to have Brenda leave.

"I'll skip the wheelchair ride," Brenda decided. "I'd be finished if she came in and found me bombing around in here, after that catastrophe."

Both girls thought about the long distance that would be between them from now on. Christie bit her lip. Nothing would ever be the same for them again.

Brenda turned at the door and said, "Good-bye for now."

"Oh!" Christie suddenly remembered. "Grand-ma said you can vis-it at Christ-mas or Feb-ru-ar-y va-ca-tions. Next sum-mer, too. Tell Rus-ty I'm com-ing. Kiss him for me."

The door whished shut, and already Christie missed her classmate, her neighbor, her best friend.

11

Two Surprises

Monday flew by, and then she had only one more whole day in the hospital. She typed a note to tell Jonathan how to reach her in Sharpe, New Hampshire.

Tuesday, before Miss Whitaker went off the floor for the day, the nurses and attendants crowded into Christie's room. They brought a cake that was shaped like Grandma and Grandpa's house. Big orange letters spelled out GOOD-BYE, CHRISTIE. She was kissed and hugged and given funny words of advice like, "Keep your nose clean." "Don't take any wooden nickels." "Don't do anything I wouldn't do." "Keep your eyes peeled." The weirdest one was, "Watch out for black cats; they're dirty."

Miss Whitaker stayed after everyone else had left. "I'll see you tomorrow morning, but there won't be time for partying, you'll be so busy getting ready to go. Don't forget, when you come to see Dr. Alexander every month, be sure to visit us on the third floor."

When she was alone, the queasy feeling in Christie's stomach made her want to throw up, but the arrival of Mark and Ellen took her mind off that. It wasn't even her therapy day, and they had made a special trip to see her.

Later, back in bed, Christie shut her eyes. What was the matter with her? She didn't want to go home. But she couldn't tell anyone that—nobody ever wanted to stay in a hospital. Out loud, she said, "I do."

In the morning she pretended to be excited. To tell the truth, the day had come all too soon for her, and everyone who came to say good-bye was too jolly. Before she was ready, she had been dressed in a new outfit and her Dartmouth sweat shirt and lifted into her wheelchair. She was glad of one thing. They hadn't stuck those creepy sneakers on her feet. She wore red, sheepskin-lined slippers over her knee socks. Nobody could see them, though, because she had a crocheted afghan over her knees and around her legs.

At about nine o'clock, Jonathan Peters rolled his wheelchair into her room. Surprised, she blurted out, "You're not su-posed to be here. You're in Mas-sa-chu-setts!"

He grinned. "I came home for two days to visit my family—and I had to come see you off."

"You said *s*!"

"Yes! They had the right key at that rehabilitation center."

She noticed that his hand was still bent, but she didn't mention it.

"I called your grandpa to find out when you would leave, and Miss Whitaker let me in early. We have time for a special journey before you go."

At the elevator, they waited for the lighted numbers to show *3,* then bumped their wheelchairs over the metal grooves. The doors glided shut, and Jonathan pushed the *1* button. On the first floor he turned left, then he guided his wheelchair along a wide corridor. They passed offices where people bustled around, typing, copying papers, talking, and laughing.

"Here we are," Jonathan said. They entered a small room with two rows of benches on either side of a red carpeted aisle.

Christie stopped her wheelchair beside his, at the entrance to the aisle.

"This is a lit-tle church," she said.

"It's a chapel," Jonathan told her.

Neither talked while Christie looked around. A soft glow from the stained glass window, directly in front of her, lit the room.

"That's the Good Shepherd." Jonathan said no more, and Christie gazed at the scene. From Sunday school, she knew that the Good Shepherd was Jesus. He was leaning forward, His hand stretched down, His fingers almost touching a small lamb on a rock ledge below Him. The little creature stood on three legs, his right front foot dangling uselessly under him.

From outside, the sunlight lit the soft colors of the window scene, the blue sky, the green grass, and tiny yellow wildflowers. The Shepherd's face was turned away. Christie could see only the back of His head, but she knew the little lamb could see His face, and in the small animal's eyes was complete trust.

Jonathan said, "There's a great peace in that window, Christie. When I was in this hospital, I used to ask to be left alone here for a while. I thought a lot about God after my accident."

Christie looked at him in surprise. He'd never said anything about God before.

His brown eyes glowed. "You know that little necklace I gave you?"

Christie nodded, and one hand went to her throat. *I can do anything.*

"Well, there's a Bible verse that says the same thing, only better: *I can do all things through Christ which strengtheneth me.* Isn't it great? At first I wondered what *all things* meant. What if I never walk again? What if my hand never straightens out?"

He held up the hand that was still bent at the wrist and stared at it. "After a while I learned that God has a plan for my life, and the tools He's given me—even this hand—are just right for what He wants me to do."

"Still speech ther-a-pist?" Christie asked.

Jonathan nodded. "I think so. But God will show me, so I'm not going to worry about it."

He looked back at the window, and Christie followed his gaze. He reached for her hand. "Store in your mind this picture of the Good Shepherd and His lamb, so you can see it when you need it—like your calendar picture. The little lamb is injured, just as we are, but see, he feels safe now. And he knows that the Shepherd is strong enough for both of them."

Christie sat quietly, wanting him to say more. His hand covered hers, resting on the arm of her wheelchair. Then he added, "And, Christie, get to know God for yourself. He'll show you His plan for your life. That's the most important thing."

"But Doc Al said the first most im-por-tant thing is re-mem-ber that mir-a-cles still hap-pen."

Jonathan nodded. "That's right. But who makes the miracles? Knowing Him is the *best* most important thing."

Christie felt the tears prickling behind her eyelids. "Thanks, Jon-a-than," she said.

"We'll do a lot of letter writing, pal," he said. "But now I'd better get you back to the lobby. Your grandpa will be waiting."

For a minute longer Christie gazed at the Good Shepherd and the little lamb, then she backed her wheelchair and turned it to follow Jonathan.

In the lobby, Grandpa and Grandma got up from the sofa as Christie and Jonathan rounded the corner of the front desk.

"All set?" Grandpa asked.

"Not quite." Grandma spoke before either of them could say anything. She went to the desk, and Christie heard her tell the receptionist, "Please buzz Miss Whitaker and Dr. Alexander. They want to see Christie off."

"The car's at the front entrance, all packed, except for two more bundles—the wheelchair and my big girl." Grandpa pointed out the front door.

When the doctor and Miss Whitaker walked out of the elevator, Christie held out her arms to the nurse. They hugged, and Miss Whitaker whispered close to Christie's ear, "I can't say this out loud, but just between you and me, you're my all-time favorite patient." She kissed the top of Christie's head. Aloud, she threatened, "You'd better visit us on checkup days, if you know what's good for you, young lady."

Dr. Alexander, then Jonathan and Miss Whitaker followed Grandpa as he pushed Christie's chair through the automatic double doors.

"This is as far as you drive, Miss Van Winkle," the doctor told her on the top step. He lifted her from the wheelchair and carried her down the two steps to the car, where the back door was already open.

Miss Whitaker and Jonathan watched from the top as Dr. Alexander ducked his head and propped Christie up against two pillows on the back seat. "Just like a queen on her throne," he said.

Grandpa put the folded wheelchair into the trunk and closed it. The doctor kissed Christie's cheek, then stepped back. Her grandparents thanked him, shook hands, waved at Miss Whitaker and Jonathan, then got into the front seat.

All this time, Christie couldn't speak. She was having trouble swallowing past the lump in her throat. But before the doctor closed her door, she called, "Bye, Doc Al; bye, Miss Whit-a-ker; bye, Jon-a-than."

They all waved, and Dr. Alexander spoke softly, "Don't forget the most important thing."

"I won't," she promised, and her gaze went to Jonathan's bright face.

Now the dreaded moment had come. The doctor pushed the door shut, Grandpa started the motor, and they were moving away from the entrance.

She couldn't really see through the blur of her tears, but she waved until Grandpa guided the car out of the driveway and onto the road. Then she leaned back against the pillows and let the tears fall. Grandpa and Grandma were very quiet.

Finally, her crying stopped. She was very tired.

When she opened her eyes, she looked into the rearview mirror, right into Grandpa's smiling face.

"There's our girl. You had yourself a good snooze," he said. "You woke up just in time to see the old mountain."

Grandma added, "We'll be home in half an hour."

Home! Christie thought. Would it ever be home to her? She turned her head to watch the view of Mt. Monadnock. Would she ever climb that mountain again with Grandpa and Benjamin and Rusty?

I can do all things.... What was the rest of that verse Jonathan had told her about? She'd have to write and ask him. And what he'd said about God's plan—that sounded interesting.

"Not far now, sweetie," said Grandpa. He looked at her in the rearview mirror. "We have a surprise for you when we get home. Two in fact."

Her heart raced, and suddenly she was wide awake. She smiled. She knew what the surprises were—Benjamin and Rusty! But she wouldn't spoil their fun.

By the time Grandpa turned into their driveway and stopped under the breezeway, Christie was ready to explode. Not a sign of Benjamin and Rusty outside. They must be hiding inside, ready to pounce out and yell and bark, "Surprise! Surprise!"

Grandpa took the folded wheelchair from the car's trunk, then lifted Christie from the back seat. "That's the way I like to see your eyes sparkle."

Christie's face felt hot as she peered at the windows and the door.

Grandpa had built a wooden ramp that covered the steps to the back porch, then another over the step to the kitchen. Grandma was already inside when Christie rolled her wheelchair into the familiar room.

She sniffed a fragrance of spice and molasses. Now she was sure. Grandma must have made Benjamin his favorite gingerbread men.

Grandpa disappeared, carrying a box of Christie's things off to her mother's old room. Grandma leaned down and whispered, "Be sure and thank Grandpa for the ramps and other changes he made for you to get around. They're your first surprise."

Disappointment hit Christie like a slap. "But maybe Rusty hasn't come yet," she told herself, "just Benjamin. The changes and Benjamin are the two surprises."

Benjamin would jump out any minute. Grandpa was probably shushing him, right now. Those two jokers! They both loved to tease. "What else could you expect from two redheads like them?" Dad always said. Grandpa's hair still had a pinkish tint to its white, and Benjamin's was almost the exact color of Rusty's coat, with darker freckles to match.

Even when Grandpa came back to the kitchen alone, Christie was alert. Jumping around the corner was too easy for them. Benjamin would be under her bed, she could almost bet on that.

"I want to look at my room," she said.

"You go ahead, I'll bring in the rest of your stuff."

Christie couldn't wait to get through the door to the hall and into Mom's room where that sneaky Benjamin waited. An unfamiliar room greeted her. Instead of Mom's bed and childhood possessions, her own maple bed, new wallpaper with pine needles, her recliner, bureau, and her desk were in place. On the desk top lay her journal. No Benjamin any- where! The bathroom door was open, and Christie could see a wooden rail on each side of the toilet.

Grandpa came in with her typewriter. Christie blurted out, "I thought Ben-ja-min was here! You said two sur-pris-es." Her voice shook.

"Why, sweetie, not yet, but we're going to call him, right now. We promised him, the minute you got settled on the sofa by the telephone."

His words destroyed any lingering hope of Benjamin's being here. Christie struggled with her anger and disappoint- ment, hating herself for being so selfish. Grandpa had worked hard to prepare this room. And Grandma had spent hours cooking—she could tell by the good smells all over the house. She hadn't even said "Thank you."

Grandpa whispered, "Be sure and tell your grandma how much you like all this. It was hard for her to let me put your mom's things in the attic and change this room. She loves you very much."

"Thanks for all your work, Grand-pa," she managed.

How could she talk to Benjamin? Knowing she was home when he was still out there in California, he would think she was a traitor, and he'd cry. How could she stand it? Why did she have to phone?

When Grandpa had lifted her to the corner of the sofa, he dialed, then handed the phone to her.

Benjamin's excited voice yelled in her ear, "Hi, Christie. You're home!"

He didn't even sound disappointed that he wasn't here. Nobody seemed to care about that but her.

Benjamin talked fast. "I'll tell you all about California when I see you again."

"O-kay, I'll write," was all Christie said. She passed the telephone to Grandpa.

"We'll talk later, old chum," Grandpa said and hung up. He didn't even hand the phone to Grandma.

Her grandparents went into the kitchen, and Christie closed her eyes. Instantly they flew open again. She heard clicking toenails on the kitchen floor, a sound she'd never forget.

"Rust-y!" she screamed as the dog bounded into the room, straight for the sofa. His front feet in her lap, and his feathery tail beating on the coffee table, he whined, yelped, and covered her face with wet dog kisses. Benjamin, a cannonball, leaped onto the sofa and landed almost on top of both of them.

While Grandpa and Grandma watched from the doorway, Benjamin shouted, "We tricked you! You thought you were calling California! I was right next door at the neighbor's all the time!"

Christie, in the midst of a tangle of dog kisses, hugs, squeals, and yelps, for the first time since the accident, felt pure joy. She leaned back and smiled her biggest smile.

Then, as though she had turned a page on her calendar, she saw a clear picture of the Good Shepherd window. "Thank You!" she whispered. "Thank You!"